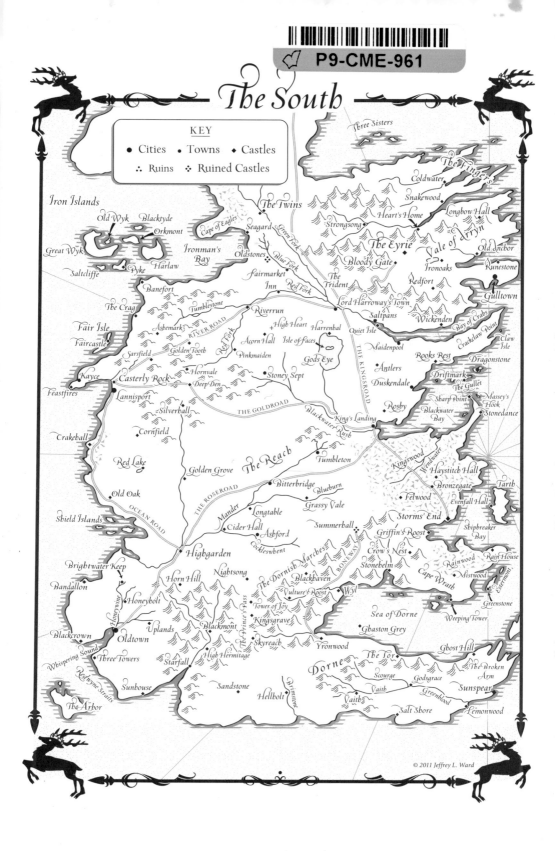

BY GEORGE R. R. MARTIN

A SONG OF ICE AND FIRE
Book One: *A Game of Thrones*
Book Two: *A Clash of Kings*
Book Three: *A Storm of Swords*
Book Four: *A Feast for Crows*
Book Five: *A Dance with Dragons*

Dying of the Light
Windhaven (with Lisa Tuttle)
Fevre Dream
The Armageddon Rag
Dead Man's Hand (with John J. Miller)

SHORT STORY COLLECTIONS
Dreamsongs, Volume I
Dreamsongs, Volume II
A Song of Lya and Other Stories
Songs of Stars and Shadows
Sandkings
Songs the Dead Men Sing
Nightflyers
Tuf Voyaging
Portraits of His Children
Quartet

EDITED BY GEORGE R. R. MARTIN
New Voices in Science Fiction, Volumes 1–4
The Science Fiction Weight-Loss Book
(with Isaac Asimov and Martin Harry Greenberg)
The John W. Campbell Awards, Volume 5
Night Visions 3
Wild Card I–XXI

A DANCE WITH DRAGONS

A DANCE
WITH
DRAGONS

BOOK FIVE OF
A SONG OF ICE AND FIRE

GEORGE R. R. MARTIN

Bantam Books | New York

A *Dance with Dragons* is a work of fiction. Names, characters, places, and incidents either are the product of the author's imagination or are used fictitiously. Any resemblance to actual persons, living or dead, events, or locales is entirely coincidental.

Copyright © 2011 by George R. R. Martin.
Endpaper and interior maps
copyright © by Jeffrey L. Ward
Heraldic crests by Virginia Norey

Published in the United States by Bantam Books, an imprint of The Random House Publishing Group, a division of Random House, Inc., New York.

BANTAM BOOKS and the rooster colophon are registered trademarks of Random House, Inc.

LIBRARY OF CONGRESS CATALOGING-IN-PUBLICATION DATA

Martin, George R. R.
A dance with dragons / George R. R. Martin.
p.   cm — (A song of ice and fire ; bk. 5)
ISBN 978-0-553-80147-7
ebook ISBN 978-0-553-90565-6
I. Title.
PS3563.A7239D36 2011
813'.54—dc22   2011015508

Printed in the United States of America on acid-free paper

www.bantamdell.com

2 4 6 8 9 7 5 3 1

First Edition

Book design by Virginia Norey

this one is for my fans

for Lodey, Trebla, Stego, Pod,
Caress, Yags, X-Ray and Mr. X,
Kate, Chataya, Mormont, Mich,
Jamie, Vanessa, Ro,
for Stubby, Louise, Agravaine,
Wert, Malt, Jo,
Mouse, Telisiane, Blackfyre,
Bronn Stone, Coyote's Daughter,
and the rest of the madmen and wild women of
the Brotherhood Without Banners

for my website wizards
Elio and Linda, lords of Westeros,
Winter and Fabio of WIC,
and Gibbs of Dragonstone, who started it all

for men and women of Asshai in Spain
who sang to us of a bear and a maiden fair
and the fabulous fans of Italy
who gave me so much wine
for my readers in Finland, Germany,
Brazil, Portugal, France, and the Netherlands
and all the other distant lands
where you've been waiting for this dance

and for all the friends and fans
I have yet to meet

thanks for your patience

A CAVIL ON CHRONOLOGY

It has been a while between books, I know. So a reminder may be in order.

The book you hold in your hands is the fifth volume of *A Song of Ice and Fire*. The fourth volume was *A Feast for Crows*. However, this volume does not follow that one in the traditional sense, so much as run in tandem with it.

Both *Dance* and *Feast* take up the story immediately after the events of the third volume in the series, *A Storm of Swords*. Whereas *Feast* focused on events in and around King's Landing, on the Iron Islands, and down in Dorne, *Dance* takes us north to Castle Black and the Wall (and beyond), and across the narrow sea to Pentos and Slaver's Bay, to pick up the tales of Tyrion Lannister, Jon Snow, Daenerys Targaryen, and all the other characters you did not see in the preceding volume. Rather than being sequential, the two books are parallel . . . divided geographically, rather than chronologically.

But only up to a point.

A Dance with Dragons is a longer book than *A Feast for Crows*, and covers a longer time period. In the latter half of this volume, you will notice certain of the viewpoint characters from *A Feast for Crows* popping up again. And that means just what you think it means: the narrative has moved past the time frame of *Feast*, and the two streams have once again rejoined each other.

Next up, *The Winds of Winter*. Wherein, I hope, everybody will be shivering together once again. . . .

—George R. R. Martin
April 2011

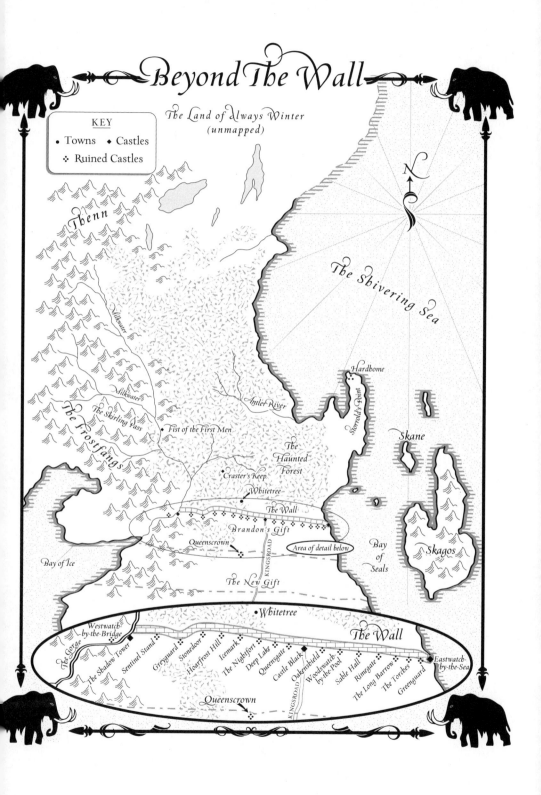

Beyond The Wall

The Land of Always Winter
(unmapped)

N

Thenn

The Shivering Sea

Milkwater

Hardhome

Antler River

The Skirling Pass

Milkwater

Storrold's Point

The Frostfangs

● Fist of the First Men

Skane

The
Haunted
Forest

● Craster's Keep

● Whitetree

Skagos

The Wall

Brandon's Gift

Bay
of
Seals

Queenscrown

Area of detail below

Bay of Ice

The New Gift

KINGSROAD

● Whitetree

The Wall

Westwatch-
by-the-Bridge

The Gorge

The Shadow Tower

Sentinel Stand

Greyguard

Stonedoor

Hoarfrost Hill

Icemark

The Nightfort

Deep Lake

Queensgate

Castle Black

Oakenshield

Woodswatch-
by-the-Pool

Sable Hall

Rimegate

The Long Barrow

The Torches

Greenguard

Eastwatch-
by-the-Sea

KINGSROAD

Queenscrown

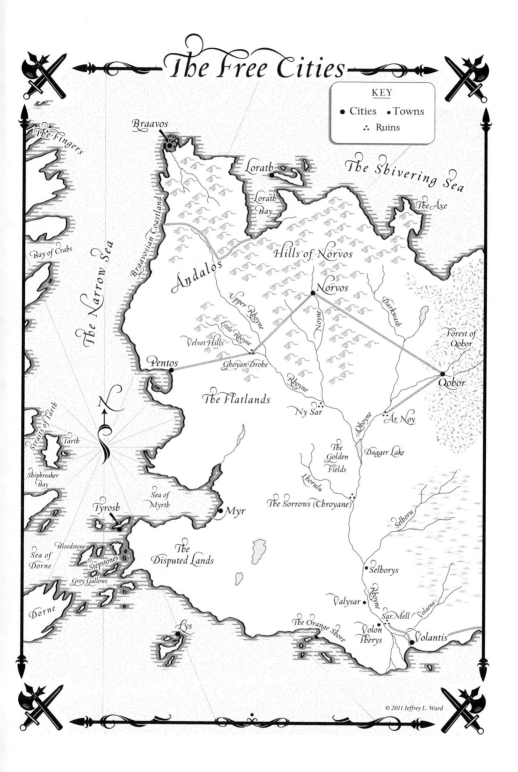

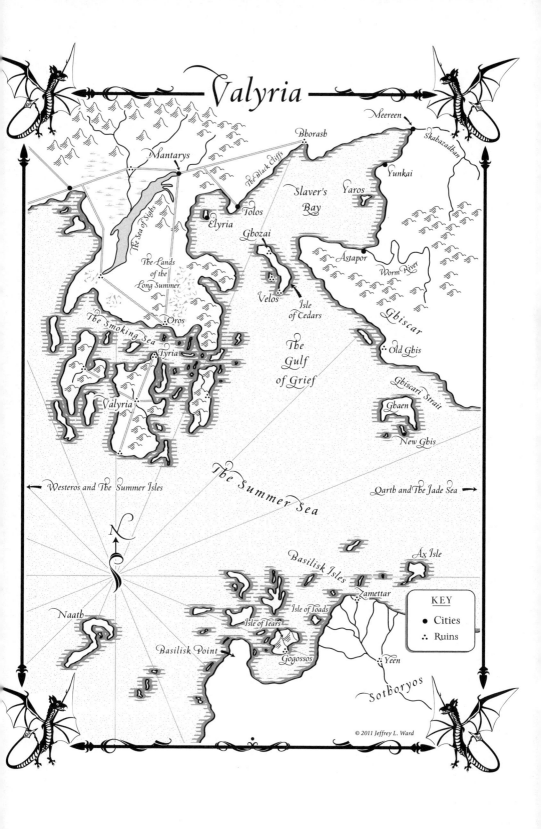

A DANCE WITH DRAGONS

PROLOGUE

The night was rank with the smell of man.

The warg stopped beneath a tree and sniffed, his grey-brown fur dappled by shadow. A sigh of piney wind brought the man-scent to him, over fainter smells that spoke of fox and hare, seal and stag, even wolf. Those were man-smells too, the warg knew; the stink of old skins, dead and sour, near drowned beneath the stronger scents of smoke and blood and rot. Only man stripped the skins from other beasts and wore their hides and hair.

Wargs have no fear of man, as wolves do. Hate and hunger coiled in his belly, and he gave a low growl, calling to his one-eyed brother, to his small sly sister. As he raced through the trees, his packmates followed hard on his heels. They had caught the scent as well. As he ran, he saw through their eyes too and glimpsed himself ahead. The breath of the pack puffed warm and white from long grey jaws. Ice had frozen between their paws, hard as stone, but the hunt was on now, the prey ahead. *Flesh*, the warg thought, *meat*.

A man alone was a feeble thing. Big and strong, with good sharp eyes, but dull of ear and deaf to smells. Deer and elk and even hares were faster, bears and boars fiercer in a fight. But men in packs were dangerous. As the wolves closed on the prey, the warg heard the wailing of a pup, the crust of last night's snow breaking under clumsy man-paws, the rattle of hardskins and the long grey claws men carried.

Swords, a voice inside him whispered, *spears*.

The trees had grown icy teeth, snarling down from the bare brown branches. One Eye ripped through the undergrowth, spraying snow. His packmates followed. Up a hill and down the slope beyond, until the wood opened before them and the men were there. One was female. The fur-wrapped bundle she clutched was her pup. *Leave her for last*, the voice whispered, *the males are the danger.* They were roaring at each other as men did, but the warg could smell their terror. One had a wooden tooth as tall as he was. He flung it, but his hand was shaking and the tooth sailed high.

Then the pack was on them.

His one-eyed brother knocked the tooth-thrower back into a snowdrift and tore his throat out as he struggled. His sister slipped behind the other male and took him from the rear. That left the female and her pup for him.

She had a tooth too, a little one made of bone, but she dropped it when the warg's jaws closed around her leg. As she fell, she wrapped both arms around her noisy pup. Underneath her furs the female was just skin and bones, but her dugs were full of milk. The sweetest meat was on the pup. The wolf saved the choicest parts for his brother. All around the carcasses, the frozen snow turned pink and red as the pack filled its bellies.

Leagues away, in a one-room hut of mud and straw with a thatched roof and a smoke hole and a floor of hard-packed earth, Varamyr shivered and coughed and licked his lips. His eyes were red, his lips cracked, his throat dry and parched, but the taste of blood and fat filled his mouth, even as his swollen belly cried for nourishment. A *child's flesh,* he thought, re-membering Bump. *Human meat.* Had he sunk so low as to hunger after human meat? He could almost hear Haggon growling at him. "Men may eat the flesh of beasts and beasts the flesh of men, but the man who eats the flesh of man is an abomination."

Abomination. That had always been Haggon's favorite word. *Abomina-tion, abomination, abomination.* To eat of human meat was abomination, to mate as wolf with wolf was abomination, and to seize the body of an-other man was the worst abomination of all. *Haggon was weak, afraid of his own power. He died weeping and alone when I ripped his second life from him.* Varamyr had devoured his heart himself. *He taught me much and more, and the last thing I learned from him was the taste of human flesh.*

That was as a wolf, though. He had never eaten the meat of men with human teeth. He would not grudge his pack their feast, however. The wolves were as famished as he was, gaunt and cold and hungry, and the prey . . . *two men and a woman, a babe in arms, fleeing from defeat to death. They would have perished soon in any case, from exposure or starva-tion. This way was better, quicker. A mercy.*

"A mercy," he said aloud. His throat was raw, but it felt good to hear a human voice, even his own. The air smelled of mold and damp, the ground was cold and hard, and his fire was giving off more smoke than heat. He moved as close to the flames as he dared, coughing and shivering by turns, his side throbbing where his wound had opened. Blood had soaked his breeches to the knee and dried into a hard brown crust.

Thistle had warned him that might happen. "I sewed it up the best I could," she'd said, "but you need to rest and let it mend, or the flesh will tear open again."

Thistle had been the last of his companions, a spearwife tough as an old root, warty, windburnt, and wrinkled. The others had deserted them along the way. One by one they fell behind or forged ahead, making for their old villages, or the Milkwater, or Hardhome, or a lonely death in the woods. Varamyr did not know, and could not care. *I should have taken one of them when I had the chance. One of the twins, or the big man with the scarred face, or the youth with the red hair.* He had been afraid, though. One of the others might have realized what was happening. Then they would have turned on him and killed him. And Haggon's words had haunted him, and so the chance had passed.

After the battle there had been thousands of them struggling through the forest, hungry, frightened, fleeing the carnage that had descended on them at the Wall. Some had talked of returning to the homes that they'd abandoned, others of mounting a second assault upon the gate, but most were lost, with no notion of where to go or what to do. They had escaped the black-cloaked crows and the knights in their grey steel, but more relentless enemies stalked them now. Every day left more corpses by the trails. Some died of hunger, some of cold, some of sickness. Others were slain by those who had been their brothers-in-arms when they marched south with Mance Rayder, the King-Beyond-the-Wall.

Mance is fallen, the survivors told each other in despairing voices, *Mance is taken, Mance is dead.* "Harma's dead and Mance is captured, the rest run off and left us," Thistle had claimed, as she was sewing up his wound. "Tormund, the Weeper, Sixskins, all them brave raiders. Where are they now?"

She does not know me, Varamyr realized then, *and why should she?* Without his beasts he did not look like a great man. *I was Varamyr Six-skins, who broke bread with Mance Rayder.* He had named himself Varamyr when he was ten. *A name fit for a lord, a name for songs, a mighty name, and fearsome.* Yet he had run from the crows like a frightened rabbit. The terrible Lord Varamyr had gone craven, but he could not bear that she should know that, so he told the spearwife that his name was Haggon. Afterward he wondered why *that* name had come to his lips, of all those he might have chosen. *I ate his heart and drank his blood, and still he haunts me.*

One day, as they fled, a rider came galloping through the woods on a gaunt white horse, shouting that they all should make for the Milkwater, that the Weeper was gathering warriors to cross the Bridge of Skulls and take the Shadow Tower. Many followed him; more did not. Later, a dour warrior in fur and amber went from cookfire to cookfire, urging all the survivors to head north and take refuge in the valley of the Thenns. Why he thought they would be safe there when the Thenns themselves had fled the place Varamyr never learned, but hundreds followed him. Hundreds more went off with the woods witch who'd had a vision of a fleet of ships coming to carry the free folk south. "We must seek the sea," cried Mother Mole, and her followers turned east.

Varamyr might have been amongst them if only he'd been stronger. The sea was grey and cold and far away, though, and he knew that he would never live to see it. He was nine times dead and dying, and this would be his true death. *A squirrel-skin cloak,* he remembered, *he knifed me for a squirrel-skin cloak.*

Its owner had been dead, the back of her head smashed into red pulp flecked with bits of bone, but her cloak looked warm and thick. It was snowing, and Varamyr had lost his own cloaks at the Wall. His sleeping pelts and woolen smallclothes, his sheepskin boots and fur-lined gloves, his store of mead and hoarded food, the hanks of hair he took from the women he bedded, even the golden arm rings Mance had given him, all lost and left behind. *I burned and I died and then I ran, half-mad with pain and terror.* The memory still shamed him, but he had not been alone. Others had run as well, hundreds of them, thousands. *The battle was lost. The knights had come, invincible in their steel, killing everyone who stayed to fight. It was run or die.*

Death was not so easily outrun, however. So when Varamyr came upon the dead woman in the wood, he knelt to strip the cloak from her, and never saw the boy until he burst from hiding to drive the long bone knife into his side and rip the cloak out of his clutching fingers. "His mother," Thistle told him later, after the boy had run off. "It were his mother's cloak, and when he saw you robbing her . . ."

"She was dead," Varamyr said, wincing as her bone needle pierced his flesh. "Someone smashed her head. Some crow."

"No crow. Hornfoot men. I saw it." Her needle pulled the gash in his side closed. "Savages, and who's left to tame them?" *No one. If Mance is dead, the free folk are doomed.* The Thenns, giants, and the Hornfoot men, the cave-dwellers with their filed teeth, and the men of the western shore with their chariots of bone . . . all of them were doomed as well. Even the crows. They might not know it yet, but those black-cloaked bastards would perish with the rest. The enemy was coming.

Haggon's rough voice echoed in his head. "You will die a dozen deaths, boy, and every one will hurt . . . but when your true death comes, you will live again. The second life is simpler and sweeter, they say."

Varamyr Sixskins would know the truth of that soon enough. He could taste his true death in the smoke that hung acrid in the air, feel it in the heat beneath his fingers when he slipped a hand under his clothes to touch his wound. The chill was in him too, though, deep down in his bones. This time it would be cold that killed him.

His last death had been by fire. *I burned.* At first, in his confusion, he thought some archer on the Wall had pierced him with a flaming arrow . . . but the fire had been *inside* him, consuming him. And the pain . . .

Varamyr had died nine times before. He had died once from a spear thrust, once with a bear's teeth in his throat, and once in a wash of blood as he brought forth a stillborn cub. He died his first death when he was only six, as his father's axe crashed through his skull. Even that had not been so agonizing as the fire in his guts, crackling along his wings, *devouring* him. When he tried to fly from it, his terror fanned the flames and made them burn hotter. One moment he had been soaring above the Wall, his eagle's eyes marking the movements of the men below. Then the flames had turned his heart into a blackened cinder and sent his spirit screaming back into his own skin, and for a little while he'd gone mad. Even the memory was enough to make him shudder.

That was when he noticed that his fire had gone out.

Only a grey-and-black tangle of charred wood remained, with a few embers glowing in the ashes. *There's still smoke, it just needs wood.* Gritting his teeth against the pain, Varamyr crept to the pile of broken branches Thistle had gathered before she went off hunting, and tossed a few sticks onto the ashes. "Catch," he croaked. "*Burn.*" He blew upon the embers and said a wordless prayer to the nameless gods of wood and hill and field.

The gods gave no answer. After a while, the smoke ceased to rise as well. Already the little hut was growing colder. Varamyr had no flint, no tinder, no dry kindling. He would never get the fire burning again, not by himself. "Thistle," he called out, his voice hoarse and edged with pain. "*Thistle!*"

Her chin was pointed and her nose flat, and she had a mole on one cheek with four dark hairs growing from it. An ugly face, and hard, yet he would have given much to glimpse it in the door of the hut. *I should have taken her before she left.* How long had she been gone? Two days? Three? Varamyr was uncertain. It was dark inside the hut, and he had been drifting in and out of sleep, never quite sure if it was day or night outside. "Wait," she'd said. "I will be back with food." So like a fool he'd waited, dreaming of Haggon and Bump and all the wrongs he had done in his long life, but days and nights had passed and Thistle had not returned. *She won't be coming back.* Varamyr wondered if he had given himself away. Could she tell what he was thinking just from looking at him, or had he muttered in his fever dream?

Abomination, he heard Haggon saying. It was almost as if he were here, in this very room. "She is just some ugly spearwife," Varamyr told him. "I am a great man. I am Varamyr, the warg, the skinchanger, it is not right that she should live and I should die." No one answered. There was no one there. Thistle was gone. She had abandoned him, the same as all the rest.

His own mother had abandoned him as well. *She cried for Bump, but she never cried for me.* The morning his father pulled him out of bed to deliver him to Haggon, she would not even look at him. He had shrieked and kicked as he was dragged into the woods, until his father slapped him and told him to be quiet. "You belong with your own kind," was all he said when he flung him down at Haggon's feet.

He was not wrong, Varamyr thought, shivering. *Haggon taught me much and more. He taught me how to hunt and fish, how to butcher a carcass and bone a fish, how to find my way through the woods. And he taught me the way of the warg and the secrets of the skinchanger, though my gift was stronger than his own.*

Years later he had tried to find his parents, to tell them that their Lump had become the great Varamyr Sixskins, but both of them were dead and burned. *Gone into the trees and streams, gone into the rocks and earth. Gone to dirt and ashes.* That was what the woods witch told his mother, the day Bump died. Lump did not want to be a clod of earth. The boy had dreamed of a day when bards would sing of his deeds and pretty girls would kiss him. *When I am grown I will be the King-Beyond-the-Wall,* Lump had promised himself. He never had, but he had come close. Varamyr Sixskins was a name men feared. He rode to battle on the back of a snow bear thirteen feet tall, kept three wolves and a shadowcat in thrall, and sat at the right hand of Mance Rayder. *It was Mance who brought me*

*to this place. I should not have listened. I should have slipped inside my
bear and torn him to pieces.*

Before Mance, Varamyr Sixskins had been a lord of sorts. He lived
alone in a hall of moss and mud and hewn logs that had once been Haggon's, attended by his beasts. A dozen villages did him homage in bread
and salt and cider, offering him fruit from their orchards and vegetables
from their gardens. His meat he got himself. Whenever he desired a
woman he sent his shadowcat to stalk her, and whatever girl he'd cast his
eye upon would follow meekly to his bed. Some came weeping, aye, but
still they came. Varamyr gave them his seed, took a hank of their hair to
remember them by, and sent them back. From time to time, some village
hero would come with spear in hand to slay the beastling and save a sister
or a lover or a daughter. Those he killed, but he never harmed the women.
Some he even blessed with children. *Runts. Small, puny things, like
Lump, and not one with the gift.*

Fear drove him to his feet, reeling. Holding his side to staunch the seep
of blood from his wound, Varamyr lurched to the door and swept aside
the ragged skin that covered it to face a wall of white. *Snow.* No wonder it
had grown so dark and smoky inside. The falling snow had buried the hut.

When Varamyr pushed at it, the snow crumbled and gave way, still soft
and wet. Outside, the night was white as death; pale thin clouds danced
attendance on a silver moon, while a thousand stars watched coldly. He
could see the humped shapes of other huts buried beneath drifts of snow,
and beyond them the pale shadow of a weirwood armored in ice. To the
south and west the hills were a vast white wilderness where nothing moved
except the blowing snow. "Thistle," Varamyr called feebly, wondering
how far she could have gone. *"Thistle. Woman. Where are you?"*

Far away, a wolf gave howl.

A shiver went through Varamyr. He knew that howl as well as Lump
had once known his mother's voice. *One Eye.* He was the oldest of his
three, the biggest, the fiercest. Stalker was leaner, quicker, younger, Sly
more cunning, but both went in fear of One Eye. The old wolf was fear-
less, relentless, savage.

Varamyr had lost control of his other beasts in the agony of the eagle's
death. His shadowcat had raced into the woods, whilst his snow bear
turned her claws on those around her, ripping apart four men before falling to a spear. She would have slain Varamyr had he come within her
reach. The bear hated him, had raged each time he wore her skin or
climbed upon her back.

His wolves, though . . .

My brothers. My pack. Many a cold night he had slept with his wolves, their shaggy bodies piled up around him to help keep him warm. *When I die they will feast upon my flesh and leave only bones to greet the thaw come spring.* The thought was queerly comforting. His wolves had often foraged for him as they roamed; it seemed only fitting that he should feed them in the end. He might well begin his second life tearing at the warm dead flesh of his own corpse.

Dogs were the easiest beasts to bond with; they lived so close to men that they were almost human. Slipping into a dog's skin was like putting on an old boot, its leather softened by wear. As a boot was shaped to accept a foot, a dog was shaped to accept a collar, even a collar no human eye could see. Wolves were harder. A man might befriend a wolf, even break a wolf, but no man could truly *tame* a wolf. "Wolves and women wed for life," Haggon often said. "You take one, that's a marriage. The wolf is part of you from that day on, and you're part of him. Both of you will change."

Other beasts were best left alone, the hunter had declared. Cats were vain and cruel, always ready to turn on you. Elk and deer were prey; wear their skins too long, and even the bravest man became a coward. Bears, boars, badgers, weasels . . . Haggon did not hold with such. "Some skins you never want to wear, boy. You won't like what you'd become." Birds were the worst, to hear him tell it. "Men were not meant to leave the earth. Spend too much time in the clouds and you never want to come back down again. I know skinchangers who've tried hawks, owls, ravens. Even in their own skins, they sit moony, staring up at the bloody blue."

Not all skinchangers felt the same, however. Once, when Lump was ten, Haggon had taken him to a gathering of such. The wargs were the most numerous in that company, the wolf-brothers, but the boy had found the others stranger and more fascinating. Borroq looked so much like his boar that all he lacked was tusks, Orell had his eagle, Briar her shadowcat (the moment he saw them, Lump wanted a shadowcat of his own), the goat woman Grisella . . .

None of them had been as strong as Varamyr Sixskins, though, not even Haggon, tall and grim with his hands as hard as stone. The hunter died weeping after Varamyr took Greyskin from him, driving him out to claim the beast for his own. *No second life for you, old man.* Varamyr Threeskins, he'd called himself back then. Greyskin made four, though the old wolf was frail and almost toothless and soon followed Haggon into death.

Varamyr could take any beast he wanted, bend them to his will, make their flesh his own. Dog or wolf, bear or badger . . .

Thistle, he thought.

Haggon would call it an abomination, the blackest sin of all, but Haggon was dead, devoured, and burned. Mance would have cursed him as well, but Mance was slain or captured. *No one will ever know. I will be Thistle the spearwife, and Varamyr Sixskins will be dead.* His gift would perish with his body, he expected. He would lose his wolves, and live out the rest of his days as some scrawny, warty woman . . . but he would live. *If she comes back. If I am still strong enough to take her.*

A wave of dizziness washed over Varamyr. He found himself upon his knees, his hands buried in a snowdrift. He scooped up a fistful of snow and filled his mouth with it, rubbing it through his beard and against his cracked lips, sucking down the moisture. The water was so cold that he could barely bring himself to swallow, and he realized once again how hot he was.

The snowmelt only made him hungrier. It was food his belly craved, not water. The snow had stopped falling, but the wind was rising, filling the air with crystal, slashing at his face as he struggled through the drifts, the wound in his side opening and closing again. His breath made a ragged white cloud. When he reached the weirwood tree, he found a fallen branch just long enough to use as a crutch. Leaning heavily upon it, he staggered toward the nearest hut. Perhaps the villagers had forgotten something when they fled . . . a sack of apples, some dried meat, anything to keep him alive until Thistle returned.

He was almost there when his crutch snapped beneath his weight, and his legs went out from under him.

How long he sprawled there with his blood reddening the snow Varamyr could not have said. *The snow will bury me.* It would be a peaceful death. *They say you feel warm near the end, warm and sleepy.* It would be good to feel warm again, though it made him sad to think that he would never see the green lands, the warm lands beyond the Wall that Mance used to sing about. "The world beyond the Wall is not for our kind," Haggon used to say. "The free folk fear skinchangers, but they honor us as well. South of the Wall, the kneelers hunt us down and butcher us like pigs."

You warned me, Varamyr thought, *but it was you who showed me Eastwatch too.* He could not have been more than ten. Haggon traded a dozen strings of amber and a sled piled high with pelts for six skins of wine, a block of salt, and a copper kettle. Eastwatch was a better place to trade than Castle Black; that was where the ships came, laden with goods from the fabled lands beyond the sea. The crows knew Haggon as a hunter and a friend to the Night's Watch, and welcomed the news he brought of life beyond their Wall. Some knew him for a skinchanger too, but no one spoke of that. It was there at Eastwatch-by-the-Sea that the boy he'd been first began to dream of the warm south.

Varamyr could feel the snowflakes melting on his brow. *This is not so bad as burning. Let me sleep and never wake, let me begin my second life.* His wolves were close now. He could feel them. He would leave this feeble flesh behind, become one with them, hunting the night and howling at the moon. The warg would become a true wolf. *Which, though?*

Not Sly. Haggon would have called it abomination, but Varamyr had often slipped inside her skin as she was being mounted by One Eye. He did not want to spend his new life as a bitch, though, not unless he had no other choice. Stalker might suit him better, the younger male . . . though One Eye was larger and fiercer, and it was One Eye who took Sly whenever she went into heat.

"They say you forget," Haggon had told him, a few weeks before his own death. "When the man's flesh dies, his spirit lives on inside the beast, but every day his memory fades, and the beast becomes a little less a warg, a little more a wolf, until nothing of the man is left and only the beast remains."

Varamyr knew the truth of that. When he claimed the eagle that had been Orell's, he could feel the other skinchanger raging at his presence. Orell had been slain by the turncloak crow Jon Snow, and his hate for his killer had been so strong that Varamyr found himself hating the beastling boy as well. He had known what Snow was the moment he saw that great white direwolf stalking silent at his side. One skinchanger can always sense another. *Mance should have let me take the direwolf. There would be a second life worthy of a king.* He could have done it, he did not doubt. The gift was strong in Snow, but the youth was untaught, still fighting his nature when he should have gloried in it.

Varamyr could see the weirwood's red eyes staring down at him from the white trunk. *The gods are weighing me.* A shiver went through him. He had done bad things, terrible things. He had stolen, killed, raped. He had gorged on human flesh and lapped the blood of dying men as it gushed red and hot from their torn throats. He had stalked foes through the woods, fallen on them as they slept, clawed their entrails from their bellies and scattered them across the muddy earth. *How sweet their meat had tasted.* "That was the beast, not me," he said in a hoarse whisper. "That was the gift you gave me."

The gods made no reply. His breath hung pale and misty in the air. He could feel ice forming in his beard. Varamyr Sixskins closed his eyes.

He dreamt an old dream of a hovel by the sea, three dogs whimpering, a woman's tears.

Bump. She weeps for Bump, but she never wept for me.

Lump had been born a month before his proper time, and he was sick so often that no one expected him to live. His mother waited until he was almost four to give him a proper name, and by then it was too late. The whole village had taken to calling him Lump, the name his sister Meha had given him when he was still in their mother's belly. Meha had given Bump his name as well, but Lump's little brother had been born in his proper time, big and red and robust, sucking greedily at Mother's teats. She was going to name him after Father. *Bump died, though. He died when he was two and I was six, three days before his nameday.*

"Your little one is with the gods now," the woods witch told his mother, as she wept. "He'll never hurt again, never hunger, never cry. The gods have taken him down into the earth, into the trees. The gods are all around us, in the rocks and streams, in the birds and beasts. Your Bump has gone to join them. He'll be the world and all that's in it."

The old woman's words had gone through Lump like a knife. *Bump sees. He is watching me. He knows.* Lump could not hide from him, could not slip behind his mother's skirts or run off with the dogs to escape his father's fury. *The dogs.* Loptail, Sniff, the Growler. *They were good dogs. They were my friends.*

When his father found the dogs sniffing round Bump's body, he had no way of knowing which had done it, so he took his axe to all three. His hands shook so badly that it took two blows to silence Sniff and four to put the Growler down. The smell of blood hung heavy in the air, and the sounds the dying dogs had made were terrible to hear, yet Loptail still came when father called him. He was the oldest dog, and his training overcame his terror. By the time Lump slipped inside his skin it was too late.

No, Father, please, he tried to say, but dogs cannot speak the tongues of men, so all that emerged was a piteous whine. The axe crashed into the middle of the old dog's skull, and inside the hovel the boy let out a scream. *That was how they knew.* Two days later, his father dragged him into the woods. He brought his axe, so Lump thought he meant to put him down the same way he had done the dogs. Instead he'd given him to Haggon.

Varamyr woke suddenly, violently, his whole body shaking. "Get up," a voice was screaming, "get up, we have to go. There are hundreds of them." The snow had covered him with a stiff white blanket. *So cold.* When he tried to move, he found that his hand was frozen to the ground. He left some skin behind when he tore it loose. "Get up," she screamed again, "they're *coming.*"

Thistle had returned to him. She had him by the shoulders and was shaking him, shouting in his face. Varamyr could smell her breath and feel the warmth of it upon cheeks gone numb with cold. *Now,* he thought, *do it now, or die.*

He summoned all the strength still in him, leapt out of his own skin, and forced himself inside her.

Thistle arched her back and screamed.

Abomination. Was that her, or him, or Haggon? He never knew. His old flesh fell back into the snowdrift as her fingers loosened. The spear-wife twisted violently, shrieking. His shadowcat used to fight him wildly, and the snow bear had gone half-mad for a time, snapping at trees and rocks and empty air, but this was worse. "Get out, *get out!*" he heard her own mouth shouting. Her body staggered, fell, and rose again, her hands flailed, her legs jerked this way and that in some grotesque dance as his spirit and her own fought for the flesh. She sucked down a mouthful of the frigid air, and Varamyr had half a heartbeat to glory in the taste of it and the strength of this young body before her teeth snapped together and filled his mouth with blood. She raised her hands to his face. He tried to push them down again, but the hands would not obey, and she was clawing at his eyes. *Abomination,* he remembered, drowning in blood and pain and madness. When he tried to scream, she spat their tongue out.

The white world turned and fell away. For a moment it was as if he were inside the weirwood, gazing out through carved red eyes as a dying man twitched feebly on the ground and a madwoman danced blind and bloody underneath the moon, weeping red tears and ripping at her clothes. Then both were gone and he was rising, melting, his spirit borne on some cold wind. He was in the snow and in the clouds, he was a sparrow, a squirrel, an oak. A horned owl flew silently between his trees, hunting a hare; Varamyr was inside the owl, inside the hare, inside the trees. Deep below the frozen ground, earthworms burrowed blindly in the dark, and he was them as well. *I am the wood, and everything that's in it,* he thought, exulting. A hundred ravens took to the air, cawing as they felt him pass. A great elk trumpeted, unsettling the children clinging to his back. A sleeping direwolf raised his head to snarl at empty air. Before their hearts could beat again he had passed on, searching for his own, for One Eye, Sly, and Stalker, for his pack. His wolves would save him, he told himself.

That was his last thought as a man.

True death came suddenly; he felt a shock of cold, as if he had been plunged into the icy waters of a frozen lake. Then he found himself rushing over moonlit snows with his packmates close behind him. Half the world was dark. *One Eye*, he knew. He bayed, and Sly and Stalker gave echo.

When they reached the crest the wolves paused. *Thistle*, he remembered, and a part of him grieved for what he had lost and another part for what he'd done. Below, the world had turned to ice. Fingers of frost crept slowly up the weirwood, reaching out for each other. The empty village was no longer empty. Blue-eyed shadows walked amongst the mounds of snow. Some wore brown and some wore black and some were naked, their flesh gone white as snow. A wind was sighing through the hills, heavy with their scents: dead flesh, dry blood, skins that stank of mold and rot and urine. Sly gave a growl and bared her teeth, her ruff bristling. *Not men. Not prey. Not these.*

The things below moved, but did not live. One by one, they raised their heads toward the three wolves on the hill. The last to look was the thing that had been Thistle. She wore wool and fur and leather, and over that she wore a coat of hoarfrost that crackled when she moved and glistened in the moonlight. Pale pink icicles hung from her fingertips, ten long knives of frozen blood. And in the pits where her eyes had been, a pale blue light was flickering, lending her coarse features an eerie beauty they had never known in life.

She sees me.

TYRION

He drank his way across the narrow sea.

The ship was small, his cabin smaller, but the captain would not allow him abovedecks. The rocking of the deck beneath his feet made his stomach heave, and the wretched food tasted even worse when retched back up. But why did he need salt beef, hard cheese, and bread crawling with worms when he had wine to nourish him? It was red and sour, very strong. Sometimes he heaved the wine up too, but there was always more.

"The world is full of wine," he muttered in the dankness of his cabin. His father never had any use for drunkards, but what did that matter? His father was dead. He'd killed him. *A bolt in the belly, my lord, and all for you. If only I was better with a crossbow, I would have put it through that cock you made me with, you bloody bastard.*

Belowdecks, there was neither night nor day. Tyrion marked time by the comings and goings of the cabin boy who brought the meals he did not eat. The boy always brought a brush and bucket too, to clean up. "Is this Dornish wine?" Tyrion asked him once, as he pulled a stopper from a skin. "It reminds me of a certain snake I knew. A droll fellow, till a mountain fell on him."

The cabin boy did not answer. He was an ugly boy, though admittedly more comely than a certain dwarf with half a nose and a scar from eye to chin. "Have I offended you?" Tyrion asked, as the boy was scrubbing. "Were you commanded not to talk to me? Or did some dwarf diddle your mother?" That went unanswered too. "Where are we sailing? Tell me that." Jaime had made mention of the Free Cities, but had never said which one. "Is it Braavos? Tyrosh? Myr?" Tyrion would sooner have gone to Dorne. *Myrcella is older than Tommen, by Dornish law the Iron Throne is hers. I will help her claim her rights, as Prince Oberyn suggested.*

Oberyn was dead, though, his head smashed to bloody ruin by the armored fist of Ser Gregor Clegane. And without the Red Viper to urge him on, would Doran Martell even consider such a chancy scheme? *He might clap me in chains instead and hand me back to my sweet sister.* The Wall might be safer. Old Bear Mormont said the Night's Watch had need of men like Tyrion. *Mormont might be dead, though. By now Slynt may be the lord commander.* That butcher's son was not like to have forgotten who sent him to the Wall. *Do I really want to spend the rest of my life eating salt beef and porridge with murderers and thieves?* Not that the rest of his life would last very long. Janos Slynt would see to that.

The cabin boy wet his brush and scrubbed on manfully. "Have you ever visited the pleasure houses of Lys?" the dwarf inquired. "Might that be where whores go?" Tyrion could not seem to recall the Valyrian word for whore, and in any case it was too late. The boy tossed his brush back in his bucket and took his leave.

The wine has blurred my wits. He had learned to read High Valyrian at his maester's knee, though what they spoke in the Nine Free Cities . . . well, it was not so much a dialect as nine dialects on the way to becoming separate tongues. Tyrion had some Braavosi and a smattering of Myrish. In Tyrosh he should be able to curse the gods, call a man a cheat, and order up an ale, thanks to a sellsword he had once known at the Rock. *At least in Dorne they speak the Common Tongue.* Like Dornish food and Dornish law, Dornish speech was spiced with the flavors of the Rhoyne, but a man could comprehend it. *Dorne, yes, Dorne for me.* He crawled into his bunk, clutching that thought like a child with a doll.

Sleep had never come easily to Tyrion Lannister. Aboard that ship it seldom came at all, though from time to time he managed to drink sufficient wine to pass out for a while. At least he did not dream. He had dreamed enough for one small life. *And of such follies: love, justice, friendship, glory. As well dream of being tall.* It was all beyond his reach, Tyrion knew now. But he did not know where whores go.

"Wherever whores go," his father had said. *His last words, and what words they were.* The crossbow *thrummed*, Lord Tywin sat back down, and Tyrion Lannister found himself waddling through the darkness with Varys at his side. He must have clambered back down the shaft, two hundred and thirty rungs to where orange embers glowed in the mouth of an iron dragon. He remembered none of it. Only the sound the crossbow made, and the stink of his father's bowels opening. *Even in his dying, he found a way to shit on me.*

Varys had escorted him through the tunnels, but they never spoke until they emerged beside the Blackwater, where Tyrion had won a famous victory and lost a nose. That was when the dwarf turned to the eunuch and said, "I've killed my father," in the same tone a man might use to say, "I've stubbed my toe."

The master of whisperers had been dressed as a begging brother, in a moth-eaten robe of brown roughspun with a cowl that shadowed his smooth fat cheeks and bald round head. "You should not have climbed that ladder," he said reproachfully.

"Wherever whores go." Tyrion had warned his father not to say that word. *If I had not loosed, he would have seen my threats were empty. He would have taken the crossbow from my hands, as once he took Tysha from my arms. He was rising when I killed him.*

"I killed Shae too," he confessed to Varys.

"You knew what she was."

"I did. But I never knew what he was."

Varys tittered. "And now you do."

I should have killed the eunuch as well. A little more blood on his hands, what would it matter? He could not say what had stayed his dagger. Not gratitude. Varys had saved him from a headsman's sword, but only because Jaime had compelled him. *Jaime . . . no, better not to think of Jaime.*

He found a fresh skin of wine instead and sucked at it as if it were a woman's breast. The sour red ran down his chin and soaked through his soiled tunic, the same one he had been wearing in his cell. The deck was swaying beneath his feet, and when he tried to rise it lifted sideways and smashed him hard against a bulkhead. *A storm*, he realized, *or else I am even drunker than I knew.* He retched the wine up and lay in it a while, wondering if the ship would sink. *Is this your vengeance, Father? Has the Father Above made you his Hand?* "Such are the wages of the kinslayer," he said as the wind howled outside. It did not seem fair to drown the cabin boy and the captain and all the rest for something he had done, but when had the gods ever been fair? And around about then, the darkness gulped him down.

When he stirred again, his head felt like to burst and the ship was spinning round in dizzy circles, though the captain was insisting that they'd come to port. Tyrion told him to be quiet and kicked feebly as a huge bald sailor tucked him under one arm and carried him squirming to the hold, where an empty wine cask awaited him. It was a squat little cask, and a tight fit even for a dwarf. Tyrion pissed himself in his struggles, for all the good it did. He was crammed face-first into the cask with his knees pushed up against his ears. The stub of his nose itched horribly, but his arms were pinned so tightly that he could not reach to scratch it. *A palanquin fit for a man of my stature,* he thought as they hammered shut the lid. He could hear voices shouting as he was hoisted up. Every bounce cracked his head against the bottom of the cask. The world went round and round as the cask rolled downward, then stopped with a crash that made him want to scream. Another cask slammed into his, and Tyrion bit his tongue.

That was the longest journey he had ever taken, though it could not have lasted more than half an hour. He was lifted and lowered, rolled and stacked, upended and righted and rolled again. Through the wooden staves he heard men shouting, and once a horse whickered nearby. His stunted legs began to cramp, and soon hurt so badly that he forgot the hammering in his head.

It ended as it had begun, with another roll that left him dizzy and more jouncing. Outside, strange voices were speaking in a tongue he did not know. Someone started pounding on the top of the cask and the lid cracked open suddenly. Light came flooding in, and cool air as well. Tyrion gasped greedily and tried to stand, but only managed to knock the cask over sideways and spill himself out onto a hard-packed earthen floor.

Above him loomed a grotesque fat man with a forked yellow beard, holding a wooden mallet and an iron chisel. His bedrobe was large enough to serve as a tourney pavilion, but its loosely knotted belt had come undone, exposing a huge white belly and a pair of heavy breasts that sagged like sacks of suet covered with coarse yellow hair. He reminded Tyrion of a dead sea cow that had once washed up in the caverns under Casterly Rock.

The fat man looked down and smiled. "A drunken dwarf," he said, in the Common Tongue of Westeros.

"A rotting sea cow." Tyrion's mouth was full of blood. He spat it at the fat man's feet. They were in a long, dim cellar with barrel-vaulted ceilings, its stone walls spotted with nitre. Casks of wine and ale surrounded them, more than enough drink to see a thirsty dwarf safely through the night. *Or through a life.*

"You are insolent. I like that in a dwarf." When the fat man laughed, his flesh bounced so vigorously that Tyrion was afraid he might fall and crush him. "Are you hungry, my little friend? Weary?"

"Thirsty." Tyrion struggled to his knees. "And filthy."

The fat man sniffed. "A bath first, just so. Then food and a soft bed, yes?

My servants shall see to it." His host put the mallet and chisel aside. "My house is yours. Any friend of my friend across the water is a friend to Illyrio Mopatis, yes."

And any friend of Varys the Spider is someone I will trust just as far as I can throw him.

The fat man made good on the promised bath, though. No sooner did Tyrion lower himself into the hot water and close his eyes than he was fast asleep. He woke naked on a goose-down feather bed so soft it felt as if he had been swallowed by a cloud. His tongue was growing hair and his throat was raw, but his cock was as hard as an iron bar. He rolled from the bed, found a chamber pot, and commenced to filling it, with a groan of pleasure.

The room was dim, but there were bars of yellow sunlight showing between the slats of the shutters. Tyrion shook the last drops off and waddled over patterned Myrish carpets as soft as new spring grass. Awkwardly he climbed the window seat and flung the shutters open to see where Varys and the gods had sent him.

Beneath his window six cherry trees stood sentinel around a marble pool, their slender branches bare and brown. A naked boy stood on the water, poised to duel with a bravo's blade in hand. He was lithe and handsome, no older than sixteen, with straight blond hair that brushed his shoulders. So lifelike did he seem that it took the dwarf a long moment to realize he was made of painted marble, though his sword shimmered like true steel.

Across the pool stood a brick wall twelve feet high, with iron spikes along its top. Beyond that was the city. A sea of tiled rooftops crowded close around a bay. He saw square brick towers, a great red temple, a distant manse upon a hill. In the far distance, sunlight shimmered off deep water. Fishing boats were moving across the bay, their sails rippling in the wind, and he could see the masts of larger ships poking up along the shore. *Surely one is bound for Dorne, or for Eastwatch-by-the-Sea.* He had no means to pay for passage, though, nor was he made to pull an oar. *I suppose I could sign on as a cabin boy and earn my way by letting the crew bugger me up and down the narrow sea.*

He wondered where he was. *Even the air smells different here.* Strange spices scented the chilly autumn wind, and he could hear faint cries drifting over the wall from the streets beyond. It sounded something like Valyrian, but he did not recognize more than one word in five. *Not Braavos,* he concluded, *nor Tyrosh.* Those bare branches and the chill in the air argued against Lys and Myr and Volantis as well.

When he heard the door opening behind him, Tyrion turned to confront his fat host. "This is Pentos, yes?"

"Just so. Where else?"

Pentos. Well, it was not King's Landing, that much could be said for it. "Where do whores go?" he heard himself ask.

"Whores are found in brothels here, as in Westeros. You will have no need of such, my little friend. Choose from amongst my servingwomen. None will dare refuse you."

"Slaves?" the dwarf asked pointedly.

The fat man stroked one of the prongs of his oiled yellow beard, a gesture Tyrion found remarkably obscene. "Slavery is forbidden in Pentos, by the terms of the treaty the Braavosi imposed on us a hundred years ago. Still, they will not refuse you." Illyrio gave a ponderous half bow. "But now my little friend must excuse me. I have the honor to be a magister of this great city, and the prince has summoned us to session." He smiled, showing a mouth full of crooked yellow teeth. "Explore the manse and grounds as you like, but on no account stray beyond the walls. It is best that no man knows that you were here."

"*Were?* Have I gone somewhere?"

"Time enough to speak of that this evening. My little friend and I shall eat and drink and make great plans, yes?"

"Yes, my fat friend," Tyrion replied. *He thinks to use me for his profit.* It was all profit with the merchant princes of the Free Cities. "Spice soldiers and cheese lords," his lord father called them, with contempt. Should a day ever dawn when Illyrio Mopatis saw more profit in a dead dwarf than a live one, Tyrion would find himself packed into another wine cask by dusk. *It would be well if I was gone before that day arrives.* That it would arrive he did not doubt; Cersei was not like to forget him, and even Jaime might be vexed to find a quarrel in Father's belly.

A light wind was riffling the waters of the pool below, all around the naked swordsman. It reminded him of how Tysha would riffle his hair during the false spring of their marriage, before he helped his father's guardsmen rape her. He had been thinking of those guardsmen during his flight, trying to recall how many there had been. You would think he might remember that, but no. A dozen? A score? A hundred? He could not say. They had all been grown men, tall and strong . . . though all men were tall to a dwarf of thirteen years. *Tysha knew their number.* Each of them had given her a silver stag, so she would only need to count the coins. *A silver for each and a gold for me.* His father had insisted that he pay her too. *A Lannister always pays his debts.*

"Wherever whores go," he heard Lord Tywin say once more, and once more the bowstring *thrum*med.

The magister had invited him to explore the manse. He found clean clothes in a cedar chest inlaid with lapis and mother-of-pearl. The clothes had been made for a small boy, he realized as he struggled into them. The fabrics were rich enough, if a little musty, but the cut was too long in the legs and too short in the arms, with a collar that would have turned his face as black as Joffrey's had he somehow contrived to get it fastened. Moths had been at them too. *At least they do not stink of vomit.*

Tyrion began his explorations with the kitchen, where two fat women and a potboy watched him warily as he helped himself to cheese, bread, and figs. "Good morrow to you, fair ladies," he said with a bow. "Do you know where whores go?" When they did not respond, he repeated the question in High Valyrian, though he had to say *courtesan* in place of *whore.* The younger, fatter cook gave him a shrug that time.

He wondered what they would do if he took them by the hand and dragged them to his bedchamber. *None will dare refuse you,* Illyrio claimed, but somehow Tyrion did not think he meant these two. The younger woman was old enough to be his mother, and the older was likely *her* mother. Both were near as fat as Illyrio, with teats that were larger than his head. *I could smother myself in flesh.* There were worse ways to die. The way his lord father had died, for one. *I should have made him shit a little gold before expiring.* Lord Tywin might have been niggardly with his approval and affection, but he had always been open-handed when it came to coin. *The only thing more pitiful than a dwarf without a nose is a dwarf without a nose who has no gold.*

Tyrion left the fat women to their loaves and kettles and went in search of the cellar where Illyrio had decanted him the night before. It was not hard to find. There was enough wine there to keep him drunk for a hundred years; sweet reds from the Reach and sour reds from Dorne, pale Pentoshi ambers, the green nectar of Myr, three score casks of Arbor gold, even wines from the fabled east, from Qarth and Yi Ti and Asshai by the Shadow. In the end, Tyrion chose a cask of strongwine marked as the private stock of Lord Runceford Redwyne, the grandfather of the present Lord of the Arbor. The taste of it was languorous and heady on the tongue, the color a purple so dark that it looked almost black in the dim-lit cellar. Tyrion filled a cup, and a flagon for good measure, and carried them up to the gardens to drink beneath those cherry trees he'd seen.

As it happened, he left by the wrong door and never found the pool he had spied from his window, but it made no matter. The gardens behind the manse were just as pleasant, and far more extensive. He wandered through them for a time, drinking. The walls would have shamed any proper castle, and the ornamental iron spikes along the top looked strangely naked without heads to adorn them. Tyrion pictured how his sister's head might look up there, with tar in her golden hair and flies buzzing in and out of her mouth. *Yes, and Jaime must have the spike beside her,* he decided. *No one must ever come between my brother and my sister.*

With a rope and a grapnel he might be able to get over that wall. He had strong arms and he did not weigh much. He should be able to clamber over, if he did not impale himself on a spike. *I will search for a rope on the morrow,* he resolved.

He saw three gates during his wanderings—the main entrance with its gatehouse, a postern by the kennels, and a garden gate hidden behind a tangle of pale ivy. The last was chained, the others guarded. The guards were plump, their faces as smooth as babies' bottoms, and every man of them wore a spiked bronze cap. Tyrion knew eunuchs when he saw them. He knew their sort by reputation. They feared nothing and felt no pain, it was said, and were loyal to their masters unto death. *I could make good use of a few hundred of mine own,* he reflected. *A pity I did not think of that before I became a beggar.*

He walked along a pillared gallery and through a pointed arch, and found himself in a tiled courtyard where a woman was washing clothes at a well. She looked to be his own age, with dull red hair and a broad face dotted by freckles. "Would you like some wine?" he asked her. She looked at him uncertainly. "I have no cup for you, we'll have to share." The washerwoman went back to wringing out tunics and hanging them to dry. Tyrion settled on a stone bench with his flagon. "Tell me, how far should I trust Magister Illyrio?" The name made her look up. "That far?" Chuckling, he crossed his stunted legs and took a drink. "I am loath to play whatever part the cheesemonger has in mind for me, yet how can I refuse him? The gates are guarded. Perhaps you might smuggle me out under your skirts? I'd be so grateful; why, I'll even wed you. I have two wives already, why not three? Ah, but where would we live?" He gave her as pleasant a smile as a man with half a nose could manage. "I have a niece in Sunspear, did I tell you? I could make rather a lot of mischief in Dorne with Myrcella. I could set my niece and nephew at war, wouldn't that be droll?" The washerwoman pinned up one of Illyrio's tunics, large enough to double as a sail. "I should be ashamed to think such evil thoughts, you're quite right. Better if I sought the Wall instead. All crimes are wiped clean when a man joins the Night's Watch, they say. Though I fear they would not let me keep you, sweetling. No women in the Watch, no sweet freckly wives to warm your bed at night, only cold winds, salted cod, and small beer. Do you think I might stand taller in black, my lady?" He filled his cup again. "What do you say? North or south? Shall I atone for old sins or make some new ones?"

The washerwoman gave him one last glance, picked up her basket, and walked away. *I cannot seem to hold a wife for very long,* Tyrion reflected. Somehow his flagon had gone dry. *Perhaps I should stumble back down to the cellars.* The strongwine was making his head spin, though, and the cellar steps were very steep. "Where do whores go?" he asked the wash flapping on the line. Perhaps he should have asked the washerwoman. *Not to imply that you're a whore, my dear, but perhaps you know where they go.* Or better yet, he should have asked his father. "Wherever whores go," Lord Tywin said. *She loved me. She was a crofter's daughter, she loved me and she wed me, she put her trust in me.*

The empty flagon slipped from his hand and rolled across the yard. Tyrion pushed himself off the bench and went to fetch it. As he did, he saw some mushrooms growing up from a cracked paving tile. Pale white they were, with speckles, and red-ribbed undersides dark as blood. The dwarf snapped one off and sniffed it. *Delicious,* he thought, *and deadly.*

There were seven of the mushrooms. Perhaps the Seven were trying to tell him something. He picked them all, snatched a glove down from the line, wrapped them carefully, and stuffed them down his pocket. The effort made him dizzy, so afterward he crawled back onto the bench, curled up, and shut his eyes.

When he woke again, he was back in his bedchamber, drowning in the goose-down feather bed once more while a blond girl shook his shoulder. "My lord," she said, "your bath awaits. Magister Illyrio expects you at table within the hour."

Tyrion propped himself against the pillows, his head in his hands. "Do I dream, or do you speak the Common Tongue?"

"Yes, my lord. I was bought to please the king." She was blue-eyed and fair, young and willowy.

"I am sure you did. I need a cup of wine."

She poured for him. "Magister Illyrio said that I am to scrub your back and warm your bed. My name—"

"—is of no interest to me. Do you know where whores go?"

She flushed. "Whores sell themselves for coin."

"Or jewels, or gowns, or castles. But where do they go?"

The girl could not grasp the question. "Is it a riddle, m'lord? I'm no good at riddles. Will you tell me the answer?"

No, he thought. *I despise riddles, myself.* "I will tell you nothing. Do me the same favor." *The only part of you that interests me is the part between your legs,* he almost said. The words were on his tongue, but somehow never passed his lips. *She is not Shae,* the dwarf told himself, *only some little fool who thinks I play at riddles.* If truth be told, even her cunt did not interest him much. *I must be sick, or dead.* "You mentioned a bath? We must not keep the great cheesemonger waiting."

As he bathed, the girl washed his feet, scrubbed his back, and brushed his hair. Afterward she rubbed sweet-smelling ointment into his calves to ease the aches, and dressed him once again in boy's clothing, a musty pair of burgundy breeches and a blue velvet doublet lined with cloth-of-gold. "Will my lord want me after he has eaten?" she asked as she was lacing up his boots.

"No. I am done with women." *Whores.*

The girl took that disappointment too well for his liking. "If m'lord would prefer a boy, I can have one waiting in his bed."

M'lord would prefer his wife. M'lord would prefer a girl named Tysha. "Only if he knows where whores go."

The girl's mouth tightened. *She despises me,* he realized, *but no more than I despise myself.* That he had fucked many a woman who loathed the very sight of him, Tyrion Lannister had no doubt, but the others had at least the grace to feign affection. *A little honest loathing might be refreshing, like a tart wine after too much sweet.*

"I believe I have changed my mind," he told her. "Wait for me abed. Naked, if you please, I'll be a deal too drunk to fumble at your clothing. Keep your mouth shut and your thighs open and the two of us should get on splendidly." He gave her a leer, hoping for a taste of fear, but all she gave him was revulsion. *No one fears a dwarf.* Even Lord Tywin had not been afraid, though Tyrion had held a crossbow in his hands. "Do you moan when you are being fucked?" he asked the bedwarmer.

"If it please m'lord."

"It might please m'lord to strangle you. That's how I served my last whore. Do you think your master would object? Surely not. He has a hundred more like you, but no one else like me." This time, when he grinned, he got the fear he wanted.

Illyrio was reclining on a padded couch, gobbling hot peppers and pearl onions from a wooden bowl. His brow was dotted with beads of sweat, his pig's eyes shining above his fat cheeks. Jewels danced when he

moved his hands; onyx and opal, tiger's eye and tourmaline, ruby, ame-
thyst, sapphire, emerald, jet and jade, a black diamond, and a green pearl.
I could live for years on his rings, Tyrion mused, *though I'd need a cleaver
to claim them.*

"Come sit, my little friend." Illyrio waved him closer.

The dwarf clambered up onto a chair. It was much too big for him, a
cushioned throne intended to accommodate the magister's massive buttocks, with thick sturdy legs to bear his weight. Tyrion Lannister had lived
all his life in a world that was too big for him, but in the manse of Illyrio
Mopatis the sense of disproportion assumed grotesque dimensions. *I am a
mouse in a mammoth's lair,* he mused, *though at least the mammoth keeps
a good cellar.* The thought made him thirsty. He called for wine.

"Did you enjoy the girl I sent you?" Illyrio asked.

"If I had wanted a girl I would have asked for one."

"If she failed to please . . ."

"She did all that was required of her."

"I would hope so. She was trained in Lys, where they make an art of
love. The king enjoyed her greatly."

"I kill kings, hadn't you heard?" Tyrion smiled evilly over his wine cup.
"I want no royal leavings."

"As you wish. Let us eat." Illyrio clapped his hands together, and serving men came running.

They began with a broth of crab and monkfish, and cold egg lime soup
as well. Then came quails in honey, a saddle of lamb, goose livers drowned
in wine, buttered parsnips, and suckling pig. The sight of it all made
Tyrion feel queasy, but he forced himself to try a spoon of soup for the
sake of politeness, and once he had tasted it he was lost. The cooks might
be old and fat, but they knew their business. He had never eaten so well,
even at court.

As he was sucking the meat off the bones of his quail, he asked Illyrio
about the morning's summons. The fat man shrugged. "There are trou-
bles in the east. Astapor has fallen, and Meereen. Ghiscari slave cities that
were old when the world was young." The suckling pig was carved. Illyrio
reached for a piece of the crackling, dipped it in a plum sauce, and ate it
with his fingers.

"Slaver's Bay is a long way from Pentos." Tyrion speared a goose liver
on the point of his knife. *No man is as cursed as the kinslayer,* he mused,
but I could learn to like this hell.

"This is so," Illyrio agreed, "but the world is one great web, and a man
dare not touch a single strand lest all the others tremble. More wine?"

Illyrio popped a pepper into his mouth. "No, something better." He clapped his hands together.

At the sound a serving man entered with a covered dish. He placed it in front of Tyrion, and Illyrio leaned across the table to remove the lid. "Mushrooms," the magister announced, as the smell wafted up. "Kissed with garlic and bathed in butter. I am told the taste is exquisite. Have one, my friend. Have two."

Tyrion had a fat black mushroom halfway to his mouth, but something in Illyrio's voice made him stop abruptly. "After you, my lord." He pushed the dish toward his host.

"No, no." Magister Illyrio pushed the mushrooms back. For a heartbeat it seemed as if a mischievous boy was peering out from inside the cheese-monger's bloated flesh. "After you. I insist. Cook made them specially for you."

"Did she indeed?" He remembered the cook, the flour on her hands, heavy breasts shot through with dark blue veins. "That was kind of her, but . . . no." Tyrion eased the mushroom back into the lake of butter from which it had emerged.

"You are too suspicious." Illyrio smiled through his forked yellow beard. Oiled every morning to make it gleam like gold, Tyrion suspected. "Are you craven? I had not heard that of you."

"In the Seven Kingdoms it is considered a grave breach of hospitality to poison your guest at supper."

"Here as well." Illyrio Mopatis reached for his wine cup. "Yet when a guest plainly wishes to end his own life, why, his host must oblige him, no?" He took a gulp. "Magister Ordello was poisoned by a mushroom not half a year ago. The pain is not so much, I am told. Some cramping in the gut, a sudden ache behind the eyes, and it is done. Better a mushroom than a sword through your neck, is it not so? Why die with the taste of blood in your mouth when it could be butter and garlic?"

The dwarf studied the dish before him. The smell of garlic and butter had his mouth watering. Some part of him wanted those mushrooms, even knowing what they were. He was not brave enough to take cold steel to his own belly, but a bite of mushroom would not be so hard. That frightened him more than he could say. "You mistake me," he heard himself say.

"Is it so? I wonder. If you would sooner drown in wine, say the word and it shall be done, and quickly. Drowning cup by cup wastes time and wine both."

"You mistake me," Tyrion said again, more loudly. The buttered mushrooms glistened in the lamplight, dark and inviting. "I have no wish to die, I promise you. I have . . ." His voice trailed off into uncertainty. *What do I have? A life to live? Work to do? Children to raise, lands to rule, a woman to love?*

"You have nothing," finished Magister Illyrio, "but we can change that." He plucked a mushroom from the butter, and chewed it lustily. "Delicious."

"The mushrooms are not poisoned." Tyrion was irritated.

"No. Why should I wish you ill?" Magister Illyrio ate another. "We must show a little trust, you and I. Come, eat." He clapped his hands again. "We have work to do. My little friend must keep his strength up."

The serving men brought out a heron stuffed with figs, veal cutlets blanched with almond milk, creamed herring, candied onions, foul-smelling cheeses, plates of snails and sweetbreads, and a black swan in her plumage. Tyrion refused the swan, which reminded him of a supper with his sister. He helped himself to heron and herring, though, and a few of the sweet onions. And the serving men filled his wine cup anew each time he emptied it.

"You drink a deal of wine for such a little man."

"Kinslaying is dry work. It gives a man a thirst."

The fat man's eyes glittered like the gemstones on his fingers. "There are those in Westeros who would say that killing Lord Lannister was merely a good beginning."

"They had best not say it in my sister's hearing, or they will find themselves short a tongue." The dwarf tore a loaf of bread in half. "And you had best be careful what you say of my family, magister. Kinslayer or no, I am a lion still."

That seemed to amuse the lord of cheese no end. He slapped a meaty thigh and said, "You Westerosi are all the same. You sew some beast upon a scrap of silk, and suddenly you are all lions or dragons or eagles. I can take you to a real lion, my little friend. The prince keeps a pride in his menagerie. Would you like to share a cage with them?"

The lords of the Seven Kingdoms did make rather much of their sigils, Tyrion had to admit. "Very well," he conceded. "A Lannister is not a lion. Yet I am still my father's son, and Jaime and Cersei are mine to kill."

"How odd that you should mention your fair sister," said Illyrio, between snails. "The queen has offered a lordship to the man who brings her your head, no matter how humble his birth."

It was no more than Tyrion had expected. "If you mean to take her up on it, make her spread her legs for you as well. The best part of me for the best part of her, that's a fair trade."

"I would sooner have mine own weight in gold." The cheesemonger laughed so hard that Tyrion feared he was about to rupture. "All the gold in Casterly Rock, why not?"

"The gold I grant you," the dwarf said, relieved that he was not about to drown in a gout of half-digested eels and sweetmeats, "but the Rock is mine."

"Just so." The magister covered his mouth and belched a mighty belch. "Do you think King Stannis will give it to you? I am told he is a great one for the law. Your brother wears the white cloak, so you are heir by all the laws of Westeros."

"Stannis might well grant me Casterly Rock," said Tyrion, "but for the small matter of regicide and kinslaying. For those he would shorten me by a head, and I am short enough as I stand. But why would you think I mean to join Lord Stannis?"

"Why else would you go the Wall?"

"Stannis is at the Wall?" Tyrion rubbed at his nose. "What in seven bloody hells is Stannis doing at the Wall?"

"Shivering, I would think. It is warmer down in Dorne. Perhaps he should have sailed that way."

Tyrion was beginning to suspect that a certain freckled washerwoman knew more of the Common Speech than she pretended. "My niece Myrcella is in Dorne, as it happens. And I have half a mind to make her a queen."

Illyrio smiled as his serving men spooned out bowls of black cherries in sweet cream for them both. "What has this poor child done to you that you would wish her dead?"

"Even a kinslayer is not required to slay *all* his kin," said Tyrion, wounded. "Queen her, I said. Not kill her."

The cheesemonger spooned up cherries. "In Volantis they use a coin with a crown on one face and a death's-head on the other. Yet it is the same coin. To queen her is to kill her. Dorne might rise for Myrcella, but Dorne alone is not enough. If you are as clever as our friend insists, you know this."

Tyrion looked at the fat man with new interest. *He is right on both counts. To queen her is to kill her. And I knew that.* "Futile gestures are all that remain to me. This one would make my sister weep bitter tears, at least."

Magister Illyrio wiped sweet cream from his mouth with the back of a fat hand. "The road to Casterly Rock does not go through Dorne, my little friend. Nor does it run beneath the Wall. Yet there is such a road, I tell you."

"I am an attainted traitor, a regicide, and kinslayer." This talk of roads annoyed him. *Does he think this is a game?*

"What one king does, another may undo. In Pentos we have a prince, my friend. He presides at ball and feast and rides about the city in a palanquin of ivory and gold. Three heralds go before him with the golden scales of trade, the iron sword of war, and the silver scourge of justice. On the first day of each new year he must deflower the maid of the fields and the maid of the seas." Illyrio leaned forward, elbows on the table. "Yet should a crop fail or a war be lost, we cut his throat to appease the gods and choose a new prince from amongst the forty families."

"Remind me never to become the Prince of Pentos."

"Are your Seven Kingdoms so different? There is no peace in Westeros, no justice, no faith . . . and soon enough, no food. When men are starving and sick of fear, they look for a savior."

"They may look, but if all they find is Stannis—"

"Not Stannis. Nor Myrcella." The yellow smile widened. "*Another.* Stronger than Tommen, gentler than Stannis, with a better claim than the girl Myrcella. A savior come from across the sea to bind up the wounds of bleeding Westeros."

"Fine words." Tyrion was unimpressed. "Words are wind. Who is this bloody savior?"

"A dragon." The cheesemonger saw the look on his face at that, and laughed. "A dragon with three heads."

DAENERYS

She could hear the dead man coming up the steps. The slow, measured sound of footsteps went before him, echoing amongst the purple pillars of her hall. Daenerys Targaryen awaited him upon the ebon bench that she had made her throne. Her eyes were soft with sleep, her silver-gold hair all tousled.

"Your Grace," said Ser Barristan Selmy, the lord commander of her Queensguard, "there is no need for you to see this."

"He died for me." Dany clutched her lion pelt to her chest. Underneath, a sheer white linen tunic covered her to midthigh. She had been dreaming of a house with a red door when Missandei woke her. There had been no time to dress.

"*Khaleesi,*" whispered Irri, "you must not touch the dead man. It is bad luck to touch the dead."

"Unless you killed them yourself." Jhiqui was bigger-boned than Irri, with wide hips and heavy breasts. "That is known."

"It is known," Irri agreed.

Dothraki were wise where horses were concerned, but could be utter fools about much else. *They are only girls, besides.* Her handmaids were of an age with her—women grown to look at them, with their black hair, copper skin, and almond-shaped eyes, but girls all the same. They had been given to her when she wed Khal Drogo. It was Drogo who had given her the pelt she wore, the head and hide of a *hrakkar*, the white lion of the Dothraki sea. It was too big for her and had a musty smell, but it made her feel as if her sun-and-stars was still near her.

Grey Worm appeared atop the steps first, a torch in hand. His bronze cap was crested with three spikes. Behind him followed four of his Unsullied, bearing the dead man on their shoulders. Their caps had only one spike each, and their faces showed so little they might have been cast of bronze as well. They laid the corpse down at her feet. Ser Barristan pulled back the bloodstained shroud. Grey Worm lowered the torch, so she might see.

The dead man's face was smooth and hairless, though his cheeks had been slashed open ear to ear. He had been a tall man, blue-eyed and fair of face. *Some child of Lys or Old Volantis, snatched off a ship by corsairs and sold into bondage in red Astapor.* Though his eyes were open, it was his wounds that wept. There were more wounds than she could count.

"Your Grace," Ser Barristan said, "there was a harpy drawn on the bricks in the alley where he was found . . ."

" . . . drawn in blood." Daenerys knew the way of it by now. The Sons of the Harpy did their butchery by night, and over each kill they left their mark. "Grey Worm, why was this man alone? Had he no partner?" By her command, when the Unsullied walked the streets of Meereen by night they always walked in pairs.

"My queen," replied the captain, "your servant Stalwart Shield had no duty last night. He had gone to a . . . a certain place . . . to drink, and have companionship."

"A certain place? What do you mean?"

"A house of pleasure, Your Grace."

A *brothel.* Half of her freedmen were from Yunkai, where the Wise Masters had been famed for training bedslaves. *The way of the seven sighs.* Brothels had sprouted up like mushrooms all over Meereen. *It is all they know. They need to survive.* Food was more costly every day, whilst the price of flesh grew cheaper. In the poorer districts between the stepped pyramids of Meereen's slaver nobility, there were brothels catering to every conceivable erotic taste, she knew. *Even so . . .* "What could a eunuch hope to find in a brothel?"

"Even those who lack a man's parts may still have a man's heart, Your Grace," said Grey Worm. "This one has been told that your servant Stalwart Shield sometimes gave coin to the women of the brothels to lie with him and hold him."

The blood of the dragon does not weep. "Stalwart Shield," she said, dry-eyed. "That was his name?"

"If it please Your Grace."

"It is a fine name." The Good Masters of Astapor had not allowed their slave soldiers even names. Some of her Unsullied reclaimed their birth names after she had freed them; others chose new names for themselves. "Is it known how many attackers fell upon Stalwart Shield?"

"This one does not know. Many."

"Six or more," said Ser Barristan. "From the look of his wounds, they swarmed him from all sides. He was found with an empty scabbard. It may be that he wounded some of his attackers."

Dany said a silent prayer that somewhere one of the Harpy's Sons was dying even now, clutching at his belly and writhing in pain. "Why did they cut open his cheeks like that?"

"Gracious queen," said Grey Worm, "his killers had forced the genitals of a goat down the throat of your servant Stalwart Shield. This one removed them before bringing him here."

They could not feed him his own genitals. The Astapori left him neither root nor stem. "The Sons grow bolder," Dany observed. Until now, they had limited their attacks to unarmed freedmen, cutting them down in the streets or breaking into their homes under the cover of darkness to murder them in their beds. "This is the first of my soldiers they have slain."

"The first," Ser Barristan warned, "but not the last."

I am still at war, Dany realized, *only now I am fighting shadows.* She had hoped for a respite from the killing, for some time to build and heal.

Shrugging off the lion pelt, she knelt beside the corpse and closed the dead man's eyes, ignoring Jhiqui's gasp. "Stalwart Shield shall not be forgotten. Have him washed and dressed for battle and bury him with cap and shield and spears."

"It shall be as Your Grace commands," said Grey Worm.

"Send men to the Temple of the Graces and ask if any man has come to the Blue Graces with a sword wound. And spread the word that we will pay good gold for the short sword of Stalwart Shield. Inquire of the butchers and the herdsmen, and learn who has been gelding goats of late." Perhaps some goatherd would confess. "Henceforth, no man of mine walks alone after dark."

"These ones shall obey."

Daenerys pushed her hair back. "Find these cowards for me. Find them, so that I might teach the Harpy's Sons what it means to wake the dragon."

Grey Worm saluted her. His Unsullied closed the shroud once more, lifted the dead man onto their shoulders, and bore him from the hall. Ser Barristan Selmy remained behind. His hair was white, and there were crow's-feet at the corners of his pale blue eyes. Yet his back was still unbent, and the years had not yet robbed him of his skill at arms. "Your Grace," he said, "I fear your eunuchs are ill suited for the tasks you set them."

Dany settled on her bench and wrapped her pelt about her shoulders once again. "The Unsullied are my finest warriors."

"Soldiers, not warriors, if it please Your Grace. They were made for the battlefield, to stand shoulder to shoulder behind their shields with their spears thrust out before them. Their training teaches them to obey, fearlessly, perfectly, without thought or hesitation . . . not to unravel secrets or ask questions."

"Would knights serve me any better?" Selmy was training knights for her, teaching the sons of slaves to fight with lance and longsword in the Westerosi fashion . . . but what good would lances do against cowards who killed from the shadows?

"Not in this," the old man admitted. "And Your Grace has no knights, save me. It will be years before the boys are ready."

"Then who, if not Unsullied? Dothraki would be even worse." Dothraki fought from horseback. Mounted men were of more use in open fields and hills than in the narrow streets and alleys of the city. Beyond Meereen's walls of many-colored brick, Dany's rule was tenuous at best. Thousands of slaves still toiled on vast estates in the hills, growing wheat and olives, herding sheep and goats, and mining salt and copper. Meereen's storehouses held ample supplies of grain, oil, olives, dried fruit, and salted meat, but the stores were dwindling. So Dany had dispatched her tiny *khalasar* to subdue the hinterlands, under the command of her three bloodriders, whilst Brown Ben Plumm took his Second Sons south to guard against Yunkish incursions.

The most crucial task of all she had entrusted to Daario Naharis, glib-tongued Daario with his gold tooth and trident beard, smiling his wicked smile through purple whiskers. Beyond the eastern hills was a range of rounded sandstone mountains, the Khyzai Pass, and Lhazar. If Daario could convince the Lhazarene to reopen the overland trade routes, grains could be brought down the river or over the hills at need . . . but the Lamb Men had no reason to love Meereen. "When the Stormcrows return from Lhazar, perhaps I can use them in the streets," she told Ser Barristan, "but until then I have only the Unsullied." Dany rose. "You must excuse me, ser. The petitioners will soon be at my gates. I must don my floppy ears and become their queen again. Summon Reznak and the Shavepate, I'll see them when I'm dressed."

"As Your Grace commands." Selmy bowed.

The Great Pyramid shouldered eight hundred feet into the sky, from its huge square base to the lofty apex where the queen kept her private chambers, surrounded by greenery and fragrant pools. As a cool blue dawn broke over the city, Dany walked out onto the terrace. To the west sunlight blazed off the golden domes of the Temple of the Graces, and etched deep shadows behind the stepped pyramids of the mighty. *In some of those pyramids, the Sons of the Harpy are plotting new murders even now, and I am powerless to stop them.*

Viserion sensed her disquiet. The white dragon lay coiled around a pear tree, his head resting on his tail. When Dany passed his eyes came open, two pools of molten gold. His horns were gold as well, and the scales that ran down his back from head to tail. "You're lazy," she told him, scratching under his jaw. His scales were hot to the touch, like armor left too long in the sun. *Dragons are fire made flesh.* She had read that in one of the books Ser Jorah had given her as a wedding gift. "You should be hunting with your brothers. Have you and Drogon been fighting again?" Her dragons were growing wild of late. Rhaegal had snapped at Irri, and Viserion had set Reznak's *tokar* ablaze the last time the seneschal had called. *I have left them too much to themselves, but where am I to find the time for them?*

Viserion's tail lashed sideways, thumping the trunk of the tree so hard that a pear came tumbling down to land at Dany's feet. His wings unfolded, and he half flew, half hopped onto the parapet. *He grows,* she thought as he launched himself into the sky. *They are all three growing. Soon they will be large enough to bear my weight.* Then she would fly as Aegon the Conqueror had flown, up and up, until Meereen was so small that she could blot it out with her thumb.

She watched Viserion climb in widening circles until he was lost to sight beyond the muddy waters of the Skahazadhan. Only then did Dany go back inside the pyramid, where Irri and Jhiqui were waiting to brush the tangles from her hair and garb her as befit the Queen of Meereen, in a Ghiscari *tokar.*

The garment was a clumsy thing, a long loose shapeless sheet that had to be wound around her hips and under an arm and over a shoulder, its dangling fringes carefully layered and displayed. Wound too loose, it was like to fall off; wound too tight, it would tangle, trip, and bind. Even wound properly, the *tokar* required its wearer to hold it in place with the left hand. Walking in a *tokar* demanded small, mincing steps and exquisite balance, lest one tread upon those heavy trailing fringes. It was not a garment meant for any man who had to work. The *tokar* was a *master's* garment, a sign of wealth and power.

Dany had wanted to ban the *tokar* when she took Meereen, but her advisors had convinced her otherwise. "The Mother of Dragons must don the *tokar* or be forever hated," warned the Green Grace, Galazza Galare. "In the wools of Westeros or a gown of Myrish lace, Your Radiance shall forever remain a stranger amongst us, a grotesque outlander, a barbarian conqueror. Meereen's queen must be a lady of Old Ghis." Brown Ben Plumm, the captain of the Second Sons, had put it more succinctly. "Man wants to be the king o' the rabbits, he best wear a pair o' floppy ears."

The floppy ears she chose today were made of sheer white linen, with a fringe of golden tassels. With Jhiqui's help, she wound the *tokar* about herself correctly on her third attempt. Irri fetched her crown, wrought in the shape of the three-headed dragon of her House. Its coils were gold, its wings silver, its three heads ivory, onyx, and jade. Dany's neck and shoulders would be stiff and sore from the weight of it before the day was done. *A crown should not sit easy on the head.* One of her royal forebears had said that, once. *Some Aegon, but which one?* Five Aegons had ruled the Seven Kingdoms of Westeros. There would have been a sixth, but the Usurper's dogs had murdered her brother's son when he was still a babe at the breast. *If he had lived, I might have married him. Aegon would have been closer to my age than Viserys.* Dany had only been conceived when Aegon and his sister were murdered. Their father, her brother Rhaegar, perished even earlier, slain by the Usurper on the Trident. Her brother Viserys had died screaming in Vaes Dothrak with a crown of molten gold upon his head. *They will kill me too if I allow it. The knives that slew my Stalwart Shield were meant for me.*

She had not forgotten the slave children the Great Masters had nailed up along the road from Yunkai. They had numbered one hundred sixty-three, a child every mile, nailed to mileposts with one arm outstretched to point her way. After Meereen had fallen, Dany had nailed up a like number of Great Masters. Swarms of flies had attended their slow dying, and the stench had lingered long in the plaza. Yet some days she feared that she had not gone far enough. These Meereenese were a sly and stubborn people who resisted her at every turn. They had freed their slaves, yes . . . only to hire them back as servants at wages so meagre that most could scarce afford to eat. Those too old or young to be of use had been cast into the streets, along with the infirm and the crippled. And still the Great Masters gathered atop their lofty pyramids to complain of how the dragon queen had filled their noble city with hordes of unwashed beggars, thieves, and whores.

To rule Meereen I must win the Meereenese, however much I may despise them. "I am ready," she told Irri.

Reznak and Skahaz waited atop the marble steps. "Great queen," declared Reznak mo Reznak, "you are so radiant today I fear to look on you." The seneschal wore a *tokar* of maroon silk with a golden fringe. A small, damp man, he smelled as if he had bathed in perfume and spoke a bastard form of High Valyrian, much corrupted and flavored with a thick Ghiscari growl.

"You are kind to say so," Dany answered, in the same tongue.

"My queen," growled Skahaz mo Kandaq, of the shaven head. Ghiscari hair was dense and wiry; it had long been the fashion for the men of the Slaver Cities to tease it into horns and spikes and wings. By shaving, Skahaz had put old Meereen behind him to accept the new, and his kin had done the same after his example. Others followed, though whether from fear, fashion, or ambition, Dany could not say; shavepates, they were called. Skahaz was *the* Shavepate . . . and the vilest of traitors to the Sons of the Harpy and their ilk. "We were told about the eunuch."

"His name was Stalwart Shield."

"More will die unless the murderers are punished." Even with his shaven scalp, Skahaz had an odious face—a beetled brow, small eyes with heavy bags beneath them, a big nose dark with blackheads, oily skin that looked more yellow than the usual amber of Ghiscari. It was a blunt, brutal, angry face. She could only pray it was an honest one as well.

"How can I punish them when I do not know who they are?" Dany demanded of him. "Tell me that, bold Skahaz."

"You have no lack of enemies, Your Grace. You can see their pyramids from your terrace. Zhak, Hazkar, Ghazeen, Merreq, Loraq, all the old slaving families. Pahl. Pahl, most of all. A house of women now. Bitter old women with a taste for blood. Women do not forget. Women do not forgive."

No, Dany thought, *and the Usurper's dogs will learn that, when I return to Westeros.* It was true that there was blood between her and the House of Pahl. Oznak zo Pahl had been cut down by Strong Belwas in single combat. His father, commander of Meereen's city watch, had died defending the gates when Joso's Cock smashed them into splinters. Three uncles had been among the hundred sixty three on the plaza. "How much gold have we offered for information concerning the Sons of the Harpy?" Dany asked.

"One hundred honors, if it please Your Radiance."

"One thousand honors would please us more. Make it so."

"Your Grace has not asked for my counsel," said Skahaz Shavepate, "but I say that blood must pay for blood. Take one man from each of the families I have named and kill him. The next time one of yours is slain, take two from each great House and kill them both. There will not be a third murder."

Reznak squealed in distress. "Noooo . . . gentle queen, such savagery would bring down the ire of the gods. We will find the murderers, I promise you, and when we do they will prove to be baseborn filth, you shall see."

The seneschal was as bald as Skahaz, though in his case the gods were responsible. "Should any hair be so insolent as to appear, my barber stands with razor ready," he had assured her when she raised him up. There were times when Dany wondered if that razor might not be better saved for Reznak's throat. He was a useful man, but she liked him little and trusted him less. The Undying of Qarth had told her she would be thrice betrayed. Mirri Maz Duur had been the first, Ser Jorah the second. Would Reznak be the third? The Shavepate? Daario? *Or will it be someone I would never suspect, Ser Barristan or Grey Worm or Missandei?*

"Skahaz," she told the Shavepate, "I thank you for your counsel. Reznak, see what one thousand honors may accomplish." Clutching her *tokar,* Daenerys swept past them down the broad marble stair. She took one step at a time, lest she trip over her fringe and go tumbling headfirst into court.

Missandei announced her. The little scribe had a sweet, strong voice. *"All kneel for Daenerys Stormborn, the Unburnt, Queen of Meereen, Queen of the Andals and the Rhoynar and the First Men, Khaleesi of Great Grass Sea, Breaker of Shackles, and Mother of Dragons."*

The hall had filled. Unsullied stood with their backs to the pillars, holding shields and spears, the spikes on their caps jutting upward like a row of knives. The Meereenese had gathered beneath the eastern windows. Her freedmen stood well apart from their former masters. *Until they stand together, Meereen will know no peace.* "Arise." Dany settled onto her bench. The hall rose. *That at least they do as one.*

Reznak mo Reznak had a list. Custom demanded that the queen begin with the Astapori envoy, a former slave who called himself Lord Ghael, though no one seemed to know what he was lord of.

Lord Ghael had a mouth of brown and rotten teeth and the pointed yellow face of a weasel. He also had a gift. "Cleon the Great sends these slippers as a token of his love for Daenerys Stormborn, the Mother of Dragons."

Irri slid the slippers onto Dany's feet. They were gilded leather, decorated with green freshwater pearls. *Does the butcher king believe a pair of pretty slippers will win my hand?* "King Cleon is most generous. You may thank him for his lovely gift." *Lovely, but made for a child.* Dany had small feet, yet the pointed slippers mashed her toes together.

"Great Cleon will be pleased to know they pleased you," said Lord Ghael. "His Magnificence bids me say that he stands ready to defend the Mother of Dragons from all her foes."

If he proposes again that I wed King Cleon, I'll throw a slipper at his head, Dany thought, but for once the Astapori envoy made no mention of a royal marriage. Instead he said, "The time has come for Astapor and Meereen to end the savage reign of the Wise Masters of Yunkai, who are sworn foes to all those who live in freedom. Great Cleon bids me tell you that he and his new Unsullied will soon march."

His new Unsullied are an obscene jape. "King Cleon would be wise to tend his own gardens and let the Yunkai'i tend theirs." It was not that Dany harbored any love for Yunkai. She was coming to regret leaving the Yellow City untaken after defeating its army in the field. The Wise Masters had returned to slaving as soon as she moved on, and were busy raising levies, hiring sellswords, and making alliances against her.

Cleon the self-styled Great was no better, however. The Butcher King had restored slavery to Astapor, the only change being that the former slaves were now the masters and the former masters were now the slaves.

"I am only a young girl and know little of the ways of war," she told Lord Ghael, "but we have heard that Astapor is starving. Let King Cleon feed his people before he leads them out to battle." She made a gesture of dismissal. Ghael withdrew.

"Magnificence," prompted Reznak mo Reznak, "will you hear the noble Hizdahr zo Loraq?"

Again? Dany nodded, and Hizdahr strode forth; a tall man, very slender, with flawless amber skin. He bowed on the same spot where Stalwart Shield had lain in death not long before. *I need this man,* Dany reminded herself. Hizdahr was a wealthy merchant with many friends in Meereen, and more across the seas. He had visited Volantis, Lys, and Qarth, had kin in Tolos and Elyria, and was even said to wield some influence in New Ghis, where the Yunkai'i were trying to stir up enmity against Dany and her rule.

And he was rich. Famously and fabulously rich . . .

And like to grow richer, if I grant his petition. When Dany had closed the city's fighting pits, the value of pit shares had plummeted. Hizdahr zo Loraq had grabbed them up with both hands, and now owned most of the fighting pits in Meereen.

The nobleman had wings of wiry red-black hair sprouting from his temples. They made him look as if his head were about to take flight. His long face was made even longer by a beard bound with rings of gold. His purple *tokar* was fringed with amethysts and pearls. "Your Radiance will know the reason I am here."

"Why, it must be because you have no other purpose but to plague me. How many times have I refused you?"

"Five times, Your Magnificence."

"Six now. I will not have the fighting pits reopened."

"If Your Majesty will hear my arguments . . ."

"I have. Five times. Have you brought new arguments?"

"Old arguments," Hizdahr admitted, "new words. Lovely words, and courteous, more apt to move a queen."

"It is your cause I find wanting, not your courtesies. I have heard your arguments so often I could plead your case myself. Shall I?" Dany leaned forward. "The fighting pits have been a part of Meereen since the city was founded. The combats are profoundly religious in nature, a blood sacrifice to the gods of Ghis. The *mortal art* of Ghis is not mere butchery but a display of courage, skill, and strength most pleasing to your gods. Victorious fighters are pampered and acclaimed, and the slain are honored and remembered. By reopening the pits I would show the people of Meereen that I respect their ways and customs. The pits are far-famed across the world. They draw trade to Meereen, and fill the city's coffers with coin from the ends of the earth. All men share a taste for blood, a taste the pits help slake. In that way they make Meereen more tranquil. For criminals condemned to die upon the sands, the pits represent a judgment by battle, a last chance for a man to prove his innocence." She leaned back again, with a toss of her head. "There. How have I done?"

"Your Radiance has stated the case much better than I could have hoped to do myself. I see that you are eloquent as well as beautiful. I am quite persuaded."

She had to laugh. "Ah, but I am not."

"Your Magnificence," whispered Reznak mo Reznak in her ear, "it is customary for the city to claim one-tenth of all the profits from the fighting pits, after expenses, as a tax. That coin might be put to many noble uses."

"It might . . . though if we *were* to reopen the pits, we should take our tenth *before* expenses. I am only a young girl and know little of such matters, but I dwelt with Xaro Xhoan Daxos long enough to learn that much.

Hizdahr, if you could marshal armies as you marshal arguments, you could conquer the world . . . but my answer is still *no*. For the sixth time."

"The queen has spoken." He bowed again, as deeply as before. His pearls and amethysts clattered softly against the marble floor. A very limber man was Hizdahr zo Loraq.

He might be handsome, but for that silly hair. Reznak and the Green Grace had been urging Dany to take a Meereenese noble for her husband, to reconcile the city to her rule. Hizdahr zo Loraq might be worth a careful look. *Sooner him than Skahaz.* The Shavepate had offered to set aside his wife for her, but the notion made her shudder. Hizdahr at least knew how to smile.

"Magnificence," said Reznak, consulting his list, "the noble Grazdan zo Galare would address you. Will you hear him?"

"It would be my pleasure," said Dany, admiring the glimmer of the gold and the sheen of the green pearls on Cleon's slippers while doing her best to ignore the pinching in her toes. Grazdan, she had been forewarned, was a cousin of the Green Grace, whose support she had found invaluable. The priestess was a voice for peace, acceptance, and obedience to lawful authority. *I can give her cousin a respectful hearing, whatever he desires.*

What he desired turned out to be gold. Dany had refused to compensate any of the Great Masters for the value of their slaves, but the Meereenese kept devising other ways to squeeze coin from her. The noble Grazdan had once owned a slave woman who was a very fine weaver, it seemed; the fruits of her loom were greatly valued, not only in Meereen, but in New Ghis and Astapor and Qarth. When this woman had grown old, Grazdan had purchased half a dozen young girls and commanded the crone to instruct them in the secrets of her craft. The old woman was dead now. The young ones, freed, had opened a shop by the harbor wall to sell their weavings. Grazdan zo Galare asked that he be granted a portion of their earnings. "They owe their skill to me," he insisted. "I plucked them from the auction bloc and gave them to the loom."

Dany listened quietly, her face still. When he was done, she said, "What was the name of the old weaver?"

"The slave?" Grazdan shifted his weight, frowning. "She was . . . Elza, it might have been. Or Ella. It was six years ago she died. I have owned so many slaves, Your Grace."

"Let us say Elza. Here is our ruling. From the girls, you shall have nothing. It was Elza who taught them weaving, not you. From you, the girls shall have a new loom, the finest coin can buy. That is for forgetting the name of the old woman."

Reznak would have summoned another *tokar* next, but Dany insisted that he call upon a freedman. Thereafter she alternated between the former masters and the former slaves. Many and more of the matters brought before her involved redress. Meereen had been sacked savagely after its fall. The stepped pyramids of the mighty had been spared the worst of the ravages, but the humbler parts of the city had been given over to an orgy of looting and killing as the city's slaves rose up and the starving hordes who had followed her from Yunkai and Astapor poured through the broken gates. Her Unsullied had finally restored order, but the sack left a plague of problems in its wake. And so they came to see the queen.

A rich woman came, whose husband and sons had died defending the city walls. During the sack she had fled to her brother in fear. When she returned, she found her house had been turned into a brothel. The whores had bedecked themselves in her jewels and clothes. She wanted her house back, and her jewels. "They can keep the clothes," she allowed. Dany granted her the jewels but ruled the house was lost when she abandoned it.

A former slave came, to accuse a certain noble of the Zhak. The man had recently taken to wife a freedwoman who had been the noble's bedwarmer before the city fell. The noble had taken her maidenhood, used her for his pleasure, and gotten her with child. Her new husband wanted the noble gelded for the crime of rape, and he wanted a purse of gold as well, to pay him for raising the noble's bastard as his own. Dany granted him the gold, but not the gelding. "When he lay with her, your wife was his property, to do with as he would. By law, there was no rape." Her decision did not please him, she could see, but if she gelded every man who ever forced a bedslave, she would soon rule a city of eunuchs.

A boy came, younger than Dany, slight and scarred, dressed up in a frayed grey *tokar* trailing silver fringe. His voice broke when he told of how two of his father's household slaves had risen up the night the gate broke. One had slain his father, the other his elder brother. Both had raped his mother before killing her as well. The boy had escaped with no more than the scar upon his face, but one of the murderers was still living in his father's house, and the other had joined the queen's soldiers as one of the Mother's Men. He wanted them both hanged.

I am queen over a city built on dust and death. Dany had no choice but to deny him. She had declared a blanket pardon for all crimes committed during the sack. Nor would she punish slaves for rising up against their masters.

When she told him, the boy rushed at her, but his feet tangled in his *tokar* and he went sprawling headlong on the purple marble. Strong Belwas was on him at once. The huge brown eunuch yanked him up one-handed and shook him like a mastiff with a rat. "Enough, Belwas," Dany called. "Release him." To the boy she said, "Treasure that *tokar*, for it saved your life. You are only a boy, so we will forget what happened here. You should do the same." But as he left the boy looked back over his shoulder, and when she saw his eyes Dany thought, *The Harpy has another Son.*

By midday Daenerys was feeling the weight of the crown upon her head, and the hardness of the bench beneath her. With so many still waiting on her pleasure, she did not stop to eat. Instead she dispatched Jhiqui to the kitchens for a platter of flatbread, olives, figs, and cheese. She nibbled whilst she listened, and sipped from a cup of watered wine. The figs were fine, the olives even finer, but the wine left a tart metallic aftertaste in her mouth. The small pale yellow grapes native to these regions produced a notably inferior vintage. *We shall have no trade in wine.* Besides, the Great Masters had burned the best arbors along with the olive trees.

In the afternoon a sculptor came, proposing to replace the head of the great bronze harpy in the Plaza of Purification with one cast in Dany's image. She denied him with as much courtesy as she could muster. A pike of unprecedented size had been caught in the Skahazadhan, and the fisherman wished to give it to the queen. She admired the fish extravagantly, rewarded the fisherman with a purse of silver, and sent the pike to her kitchens. A coppersmith had fashioned her a suit of burnished rings to wear to war. She accepted it with fulsome thanks; it was lovely to behold, and all that burnished copper would flash prettily in the sun, though if actual battle threatened, she would sooner be clad in steel. Even a young girl who knew nothing of the ways of war knew *that.*

The slippers the Butcher King had sent her had grown too uncomfortable. Dany kicked them off and sat with one foot tucked beneath her and the other swinging back and forth. It was not a very regal pose, but she was tired of being regal. The crown had given her a headache, and her buttocks had gone to sleep. "Ser Barristan," she called, "I know what quality a king needs most."

"Courage, Your Grace?"

"Cheeks like iron," she teased. "All I do is sit."

"Your Grace takes too much on herself. You should allow your councillors to shoulder more of your burdens."

"I have too many councillors and too few cushions." Dany turned to Reznak. "How many more?"

"Three-and-twenty, if it please Your Magnificence. With as many claims." The seneschal consulted some papers. "One calf and three goats. The rest will be sheep or lambs, no doubt."

"Three-and-twenty." Dany sighed. "My dragons have developed a prodigious taste for mutton since we began to pay the shepherds for their kills. Have these claims been proven?"

"Some men have brought burnt bones."

"Men make fires. Men cook mutton. Burnt bones prove nothing. Brown Ben says there are red wolves in the hills outside the city, and jackals and wild dogs. Must we pay good silver for every lamb that goes astray between Yunkai and the Skahazadhan?"

"No, Magnificence." Reznak bowed. "Shall I send these rascals away, or will you want them scourged?"

Daenerys shifted on the bench. "No man should ever fear to come to me." Some claims were false, she did not doubt, but more were genuine. Her dragons had grown too large to be content with rats and cats and dogs. *The more they eat, the larger they will grow*, Ser Barristan had warned her, *and the larger they grow, the more they'll eat*. Drogon especially ranged far afield and could easily devour a sheep a day. "Pay them for the value of their animals," she told Reznak, "but henceforth claimants must present themselves at the Temple of the Graces and swear a holy oath before the gods of Ghis."

"It shall be done." Reznak turned to the petitioners. "Her Magnificence the Queen has consented to compensate each of you for the animals you have lost," he told them in the Ghiscari tongue. "Present yourselves to my factors on the morrow, and you shall be paid in coin or kind, as you prefer."

The pronouncement was received in sullen silence. *You would think they might be happier*, Dany thought. *They have what they came for. Is there no way to please these people?*

One man lingered behind as the rest were filing out—a squat man with a windburnt face, shabbily dressed. His hair was a cap of coarse red-black wire cropped about his ears, and in one hand he held a sad cloth sack. He stood with his head down, gazing at the marble floor as if he had quite forgotten where he was. *And what does this one want?* Dany wondered.

"*All kneel for Daenerys Stormborn, the Unburnt, Queen of Meereen,*

Queen of the Andals and the Rhoynar and the First Men, Khaleesi *of Great Grass Sea, Breaker of Shackles, and Mother of Dragons,"* cried Missandei in her high, sweet voice.

As Dany stood, her *tokar* began to slip. She caught it and tugged it back in place. "You with the sack," she called, "did you wish to speak with us? You may approach."

When he raised his head, his eyes were red and raw as open sores. Dany glimpsed Ser Barristan sliding closer, a white shadow at her side. The man approached in a stumbling shuffle, one step and then another, clutching his sack. *Is he drunk, or ill?* she wondered. There was dirt beneath his cracked yellow fingernails.

"What is it?" Dany asked. "Do you have some grievance to lay before us, some petition? What would you have of us?"

His tongue flicked nervously over chapped, cracked lips. "I . . . I brought . . ."

"Bones?" she said, impatiently. "Burnt bones?"

He lifted the sack, and spilled its contents on the marble.

Bones they were, broken bones and blackened. The longer ones had been cracked open for their marrow.

"It were the black one," the man said, in a Ghiscari growl, "the winged shadow. He come down from the sky and . . . and . . ."

No. Dany shivered. *No, no, oh no.*

"Are you deaf, fool?" Reznak mo Reznak demanded of the man. "Did you not hear my pronouncement? See my factors on the morrow, and you shall be paid for your sheep."

"Reznak," Ser Barristan said quietly, "hold your tongue and open your eyes. Those are no sheep bones."

No, Dany thought, *those are the bones of a child.*

JON

The white wolf raced through a black wood, beneath a pale cliff as tall as the sky. The moon ran with him, slipping through a tangle of bare branches overhead, across the starry sky.

"Snow," the moon murmured. The wolf made no answer. Snow crunched beneath his paws. The wind sighed through the trees.

Far off, he could hear his packmates calling to him, like to like. They were hunting too. A wild rain lashed down upon his black brother as he tore at the flesh of an enormous goat, washing the blood from his side where the goat's long horn had raked him. In another place, his little sister lifted her head to sing to the moon, and a hundred small grey cousins broke off their hunt to sing with her. The hills were warmer where they were, and full of food. Many a night his sister's pack gorged on the flesh of sheep and cows and horses, the prey of men, and sometimes even on the flesh of man himself.

"Snow," the moon called down again, cackling. The white wolf padded along the man trail beneath the icy cliff. The taste of blood was on his tongue, and his ears rang to the song of the hundred cousins. Once they had been six, five whimpering blind in the snow beside their dead mother, sucking cool milk from her hard dead nipples whilst he crawled off alone. Four remained . . . and one the white wolf could no longer sense.

"Snow," the moon insisted.

The white wolf ran from it, racing toward the cave of night where the sun had hidden, his breath frosting in the air. On starless nights the great cliff was as black as stone, a darkness towering high above the wide world, but when the moon came out it shimmered pale and icy as a frozen stream. The wolf's pelt was thick and shaggy, but when the wind blew along the ice no fur could keep the chill out. On the other side the wind was colder still, the wolf sensed. That was where his brother was, the grey brother who smelled of summer.

"Snow." An icicle tumbled from a branch. The white wolf turned and bared his teeth. "*Snow!*" His fur rose bristling, as the woods dissolved around him. "*Snow, snow, snow!*" He heard the beat of wings. Through the gloom a raven flew.

It landed on Jon Snow's chest with a *thump* and a scrabbling of claws. "SNOW!" it screamed into his face.

"I hear you." The room was dim, his pallet hard. Grey light leaked through the shutters, promising another bleak cold day. "Is this how you woke Mormont? Get your feathers out of my face." Jon wriggled an arm out from under his blankets to shoo the raven off. It was a big bird, old and bold and scruffy, utterly without fear. "*Snow,*" it cried, flapping to his bedpost. "*Snow, snow.*" Jon filled his fist with a pillow and let fly, but the bird took to the air. The pillow struck the wall and burst, scattering stuffing everywhere just as Dolorous Edd Tollett poked his head through the door. "Beg pardon," he said, ignoring the flurry of feathers, "shall I fetch m'lord some breakfast?"

"*Corn,*" cried the raven. "*Corn, corn.*"

"Roast raven," Jon suggested. "And half a pint of ale." Having a steward fetch and serve for him still felt strange; not long ago, it would have been him fetching breakfast for Lord Commander Mormont.

"Three corns and one roast raven," said Dolorous Edd. "Very good, m'lord, only Hobb's made boiled eggs, black sausage, and apples stewed with prunes. The apples stewed with prunes are excellent, except for the prunes. I won't eat prunes myself. Well, there was one time when Hobb chopped them up with chestnuts and carrots and hid them in a hen. Never trust a cook, my lord. They'll prune you when you least expect it."

"Later." Breakfast could wait; Stannis could not. "Any trouble from the stockades last night?"

"Not since you put guards on the guards, m'lord."

"Good." A thousand wildlings had been penned up beyond the Wall, the captives Stannis Baratheon had taken when his knights had smashed Mance Rayder's patchwork host. Many of the prisoners were women, and some of the guards had been sneaking them out to warm their beds. King's men, queen's men, it did not seem to matter; a few black brothers had tried the same thing. Men were men, and these were the only women for a thousand leagues.

"Two more wildlings turned up to surrender," Edd went on. "A mother with a girl clinging to her skirts. She had a boy babe too, all swaddled up in fur, but he was dead."

"*Dead*," said the raven. It was one of the bird's favorite words. "*Dead, dead, dead.*"

They had free folk drifting in most every night, starved half-frozen creatures who had run from the battle beneath the Wall only to crawl back when they realized there was no safe place to run to. "Was the mother questioned?" Jon asked. Stannis Baratheon had smashed Mance Rayder's host and made the King-Beyond-the-Wall his captive . . . but the wildlings were still out there, the Weeper and Tormund Giantsbane and thousands more.

"Aye, m'lord," said Edd, "but all she knows is that she ran off during the battle and hid in the woods after. We filled her full of porridge, sent her to the pens, and burned the babe."

Burning dead children had ceased to trouble Jon Snow; live ones were another matter. *Two kings to wake the dragon. The father first and then the son, so both die kings.* The words had been murmured by one of the queen's men as Maester Aemon had cleaned his wounds. Jon had tried to dismiss them as his fever talking. Aemon had demurred. "There is power in a king's blood," the old maester had warned, "and better men than Stannis have done worse things than this." *The king can be harsh and unforgiving, aye, but a babe still on the breast? Only a monster would give a living child to the flames.*

Jon pissed in darkness, filling his chamber pot as the Old Bear's raven muttered complaints. The wolf dreams had been growing stronger, and he found himself remembering them even when awake. *Ghost knows that Grey Wind is dead.* Robb had died at the Twins, betrayed by men he'd believed his friends, and his wolf had perished with him. Bran and Rickon had been murdered too, beheaded at the behest of Theon Greyjoy, who had once been their lord father's ward . . . but if dreams did not lie, their direwolves had escaped. At Queenscrown, one had come out of the darkness to save Jon's life. *Summer, it had to be. His fur was grey, and Shaggydog is black.* He wondered if some part of his dead brothers lived on inside their wolves.

He filled his basin from the flagon of water beside his bed, washed his face and hands, donned a clean set of black woolens, laced up a black leather jerkin, and pulled on a pair of well-worn boots. Mormont's raven watched with shrewd black eyes, then fluttered to the window. "Do you take me for your thrall?" When Jon folded back the window with its thick diamond-shaped panes of yellow glass, the chill of the morning hit him in the face. He took a breath to clear away the cobwebs of the night as the raven flapped away. *That bird is too clever by half.* It had been the Old Bear's companion for long years, but that had not stopped it from eating Mormont's face once he died.

Outside his bedchamber a flight of steps descended to a larger room furnished with a scarred pinewood table and a dozen oak-and-leather chairs. With Stannis in the King's Tower and the Lord Commander's Tower burned to a shell, Jon had established himself in Donal Noye's modest rooms behind the armory. In time, no doubt, he would need larger quarters, but for the moment these would serve whilst he accustomed himself to command.

The grant that the king had presented him for signature was on the table beneath a silver drinking cup that had once been Donal Noye's. The one-armed smith had left few personal effects: the cup, six pennies and a copper star, a niello brooch with a broken clasp, a musty brocade doublet that bore the stag of Storm's End. *His treasures were his tools, and the swords and knives he made. His life was at the forge.* Jon moved the cup aside and read the parchment once again. *If I put my seal to this, I will forever be remembered as the lord commander who gave away the Wall,* he thought, *but if I should refuse . . .*

Stannis Baratheon was proving to be a prickly guest, and a restless one. He had ridden down the kingsroad almost as far as Queenscrown, prowled through the empty hovels of Mole's Town, inspected the ruined forts at Queensgate and Oakenshield. Each night he walked atop the Wall with Lady Melisandre, and during the days he visited the stockades, picking captives out for the red woman to question. *He does not like to be balked.* This would not be a pleasant morning, Jon feared.

From the armory came a clatter of shields and swords, as the latest lot of boys and raw recruits armed themselves. He could hear the voice of Iron Emmett telling them to be quick about it. Cotter Pyke had not been pleased to lose him, but the young ranger had a gift for training men. *He loves to fight, and he'll teach his boys to love it too.* Or so he hoped.

Jon's cloak hung on a peg by the door, his sword belt on another. He donned them both and made his way to the armory. The rug where Ghost slept was empty, he saw. Two guardsmen stood inside the doors, clad in black cloaks and iron halfhelms, spears in their hands. "Will m'lord be wanting a tail?" asked Garse.

"I think I can find the King's Tower by myself." Jon hated having guards trailing after him everywhere he went. It made him feel like a mother duck leading a procession of ducklings.

Iron Emmett's lads were well at it in the yard, blunted swords slamming into shields and ringing against one another. Jon stopped to watch a moment as Horse pressed Hop-Robin back toward the well. Horse had the makings of a good fighter, he decided. He was strong and getting stronger, and his instincts were sound. Hop-Robin was another tale. His clubfoot was bad enough, but he was afraid of getting hit as well. *Perhaps we can make a steward of him.* The fight ended abruptly, with Hop-Robin on the ground.

"Well fought," Jon said to Horse, "but you drop your shield too low when pressing an attack. You will want to correct that, or it is like to get you killed."

"Yes, m'lord. I'll keep it higher next time." Horse pulled Hop-Robin to his feet, and the smaller boy made a clumsy bow.

A few of Stannis's knights were sparring on the far side of the yard. *King's men in one corner and queen's men in another,* Jon did not fail to note, *but only a few. It's too cold for most of them.* As he strode past them, a booming voice called after him. "BOY! YOU THERE! BOY!"

Boy was not the worst of the things that Jon Snow had been called since being chosen lord commander. He ignored it.

"*Snow,*" the voice insisted, "*Lord Commander.*"

This time he stopped. "Ser?"

The knight overtopped him by six inches. "A man who bears Valyrian steel should use it for more than scratching his arse."

Jon had seen this one about the castle—a knight of great renown, to hear him tell it. During the battle beneath the Wall, Ser Godry Farring had slain a fleeing giant, pounding after him on horseback and driving a lance through his back, then dismounting to hack off the creature's pitiful small head. The queen's men had taken to calling him Godry the Giantslayer.

Jon remembered Ygritte, crying. *I am the last of the giants.* "I use Longclaw when I must, ser."

"How well, though?" Ser Godry drew his own blade. "Show us. I promise not to hurt you, lad."

How kind of you. "Some other time, ser. I fear that I have other duties just now."

"You fear. I see that." Ser Godry grinned at his friends. "He fears," he repeated, for the slow ones.

"You will excuse me." Jon showed them his back.

Castle Black seemed a bleak and forlorn place in the pale dawn light. *My command,* Jon Snow reflected ruefully, *as much a ruin as it is a strong-*

hold. The Lord Commander's Tower was a shell, the Common Hall a pile of blackened timbers, and Hardin's Tower looked as if the next gust of wind would knock it over . . . though it had looked that way for years. Behind them rose the Wall: immense, forbidding, frigid, acrawl with builders pushing up a new switchback stair to join the remnants of the old. They worked from dawn to dusk. Without the stair, there was no way to reach the top of the Wall save by winch. That would not serve if the wildlings should attack again.

Above the King's Tower the great golden battle standard of House Baratheon cracked like a whip from the roof where Jon Snow had prowled with bow in hand not long ago, slaying Thenns and free folk beside Satin and Deaf Dick Follard. Two queen's men stood shivering on the steps, their hands tucked up into their armpits and their spears leaning against the door. "Those cloth gloves will never serve," Jon told them. "See Bowen Marsh on the morrow, and he'll give you each a pair of leather gloves lined with fur."

"We will, m'lord, and thank you," said the older guard.

"That's if our bloody hands aren't froze off," the younger added, his breath a pale mist. "I used to think that it got cold up in the Dornish Marches. What did I know?"

Nothing, thought Jon Snow, *the same as me.*

Halfway up the winding steps, he came upon Samwell Tarly, headed down. "Are you coming from the king?" Jon asked him.

"Maester Aemon sent me with a letter."

"I see." Some lords trusted their maesters to read their letters and convey the contents, but Stannis insisted on breaking the seals himself. "How did Stannis take it?"

"Not happily, by his face." Sam dropped his voice to a whisper. "I am not supposed to speak of it."

"Then don't." Jon wondered which of his father's bannermen had refused King Stannis homage this time. *He was quick enough to spread the word when Karhold declared for him.* "How are you and your longbow getting on?"

"I found a good book about archery." Sam frowned. "Doing it is harder than reading about it, though. I get blisters."

"Keep at it. We may need your bow on the Wall if the Others turn up some dark night."

"Oh, I hope not."

More guards stood outside the king's solar. "No arms are allowed in His Grace's presence, my lord," their serjeant said. "I'll need that sword. Your knives as well." It would do no good to protest, Jon knew. He handed them his weaponry.

Within the solar the air was warm. Lady Melisandre was seated near the fire, her ruby glimmering against the pale skin of her throat. Ygritte had been kissed by fire; the red priestess *was* fire, and her hair was blood and flame. Stannis stood behind the rough-hewn table where the Old Bear had once been wont to sit and take his meals. Covering the table was a large map of the north, painted on a ragged piece of hide. A tallow candle weighed down one end of it, a steel gauntlet the other.

The king wore lambswool breeches and a quilted doublet, yet somehow he looked as stiff and uncomfortable as if he had been clad in plate and mail. His skin was pale leather, his beard cropped so short that it might have been painted on. A fringe about his temples was all that remained of his black hair. In his hand was a parchment with a broken seal of dark green wax.

Jon took a knee. The king frowned at him, and rattled the parchment angrily. "Rise. Tell me, who is *Lyanna Mormont?*"

"One of Lady Maege's daughters, Sire. The youngest. She was named for my lord father's sister."

"To curry your lord father's favor, I don't doubt. I know how that game is played. How old is this wretched girl child?"

Jon had to think a moment. "Ten. Or near enough to make no matter. Might I know how she has offended Your Grace?"

Stannis read from the letter. "*Bear Island knows no king but the King in the North, whose name is STARK. A girl of ten, you say, and she presumes to scold her lawful king."* His close-cropped beard lay like a shadow over his hollow cheeks. "See that you keep these tidings to yourself, Lord Snow. Karhold is with me, that is all the men need know. I will not have your brothers trading tales of how this child spat on me."

"As you command, Sire." Maege Mormont had ridden south with Robb, Jon knew. Her eldest daughter had joined the Young Wolf's host as well. Even if both of them had died, however, Lady Maege had other daughters, some with children of their own. Had they gone with Robb as well? Surely Lady Maege would have left at least one of the older girls behind as castellan. He did not understand why Lyanna should be writing Stannis, and could not help but wonder if the girl's answer might have been different if the letter had been sealed with a direwolf instead of a crowned stag, and signed by Jon Stark, Lord of Winterfell. *It is too late for such misgivings. You made your choice.*

"Two score ravens were sent out," the king complained, "yet we get no response but silence and defiance. Homage is the duty every leal subject owes his king. Yet your father's bannermen all turn their back on me, save the Karstarks. Is Arnolf Karstark the only man of honor in the north?"

Arnolf Karstark was the late Lord Rickard's uncle. He had been made the castellan of Karhold when his nephew and his sons went south with Robb, and he had been the first to respond to King Stannis's call for homage, with a raven declaring his allegiance. *The Karstarks have no other choice,* Jon might have said. Rickard Karstark had betrayed the direwolf and spilled the blood of lions. The stag was Karhold's only hope. "In times as confused as these, even men of honor must wonder where their duty lies. Your Grace is not the only king in the realm demanding homage."

Lady Melisandre stirred. "Tell me, Lord Snow . . . where were these other kings when the wild people stormed your Wall?"

"A thousand leagues away and deaf to our need," Jon replied. "I have not forgotten that, my lady. Nor will I. But my father's bannermen have wives and children to protect, and smallfolk who will die should they choose wrongly. His Grace asks much of them. Give them time, and you will have your answers."

"Answers such as this?" Stannis crushed Lyanna's letter in his fist.

"Even in the north men fear the wroth of Tywin Lannister. Boltons make bad enemies as well. It is not happenstance that put a flayed man on their banners. They north rode with Robb, bled with him, died for him. They have supped on grief and death, and now you come to offer them another serving. Do you blame them if they hang back? Forgive me, Your Grace, but some will look at you and see only another doomed pretender."

"If His Grace is doomed, your realm is doomed as well," said Lady Melisandre. "Remember that, Lord Snow. It is the one true king of Westeros who stands before you."

Jon kept his face a mask. "As you say, my lady."

Stannis snorted. "You spend your words as if every one were a golden dragon. I wonder, how much gold do you have laid by?"

"Gold?" *Are those the dragons the red woman means to wake? Dragons made of gold?* "Such taxes as we collect are paid in kind, Your Grace. The Watch is rich in turnips but poor in coin."

"Turnips are not like to appease Salladhor Saan. I require gold or silver."

"For that, you need White Harbor. The city cannot compare to Oldtown or King's Landing, but it is still a thriving port. Lord Manderly is the richest of my lord father's bannermen."

"Lord Too-Fat-to-Sit-a-Horse." The letter that Lord Wyman Manderly had sent back from White Harbor had spoken of his age and infirmity, and little more. Stannis had commanded Jon not to speak of that one either.

"Perhaps his lordship would fancy a wildling wife," said Lady Melisandre. "Is this fat man married, Lord Snow?"

"His lady wife is long dead. Lord Wyman has two grown sons, and grandchildren by the elder. And he *is* too fat to sit a horse, thirty stone at least. Val would never have him."

"Just once you might try to give me an answer that would please me, Lord Snow," the king grumbled.

"I would hope the truth would please you, Sire. Your men call Val a princess, but to the free folk she is only the sister of their king's dead wife. If you force her to marry a man she does not want, she is like to slit his throat on their wedding night. Even if she accepts her husband, that does not mean the wildlings will follow him, or you. The only man who can bind them to your cause is Mance Rayder."

"I know that," Stannis said, unhappily. "I have spent hours speaking with the man. He knows much and more of our true enemy, and there is cunning in him, I'll grant you. Even if he were to renounce his kingship, though, the man remains an oathbreaker. Suffer one deserter to live, and you encourage others to desert. No. Laws should be made of iron, not of pudding. Mance Rayder's life is forfeit by every law of the Seven Kingdoms."

"The law ends at the Wall, Your Grace. You could make good use of Mance."

"I mean to. I'll *burn* him, and the north will see how I deal with turncloaks and traitors. I have other men to lead the wildlings. And I have Rayder's son, do not forget. Once the father dies, his whelp will be the King-Beyond-the-Wall."

"Your Grace is mistaken." *You know nothing, Jon Snow,* Ygritte used to say, but he had learned. "The babe is no more a prince than Val is a princess. You do not become King-Beyond-the-Wall because your father was."

"Good," said Stannis, "for I will suffer no other kings in Westeros. Have you signed the grant?"

"No, Your Grace." *And now it comes.* Jon closed his burned fingers and opened them again. "You ask too much."

"*Ask?* I *asked* you to be Lord of Winterfell and Warden of the North. I *require* these castles."

"We have ceded you the Nightfort."

"Rats and ruins. It is a niggard's gift that costs the giver nothing. Your own man Yarwyck says it will be half a year before the castle can be made fit for habitation."

"The other forts are no better."

"I know that. It makes no matter. They are all we have. There are nineteen forts along the Wall, and you have men in only three of them. I mean to have every one of them garrisoned again before the year is out."

"I have no quarrel with that, Sire, but it is being said that you also mean to grant these castles to your knights and lords, to hold as their own seats as vassals to Your Grace."

"Kings are expected to be open-handed to their followers. Did Lord Eddard teach his bastard nothing? Many of my knights and lords abandoned rich lands and stout castles in the south. Should their loyalty go unrewarded?"

"If Your Grace wishes to lose all of my lord father's bannermen, there is no more certain way than by giving northern halls to southron lords."

"How can I lose men I do not have? I had hoped to bestow Winterfell on a northman, you may recall. A son of Eddard Stark. He threw my offer in my face." Stannis Baratheon with a grievance was like a mastiff with a bone; he gnawed it down to splinters.

"By right Winterfell should go to my sister Sansa."

"Lady Lannister, you mean? Are you so eager to see the Imp perched on your father's seat? I promise you, that will not happen whilst I live, Lord Snow."

Jon knew better than to press the point. "Sire, some claim that you mean to grant lands and castles to Rattleshirt and the Magnar of Thenn."

"Who told you that?"

The talk was all over Castle Black. "If you must know, I had the tale from Gilly."

"Who is *Gilly*?"

"The wet nurse," said Lady Melisandre. "Your Grace gave her freedom of the castle."

"Not for running tales. She's wanted for her teats, not for her tongue. I'll have more milk from her, and fewer *messages*."

"Castle Black needs no useless mouths," Jon agreed. "I am sending Gilly south on the next ship out of Eastwatch."

Melisandre touched the ruby at her neck. "Gilly is giving suck to Dalla's son as well as her own. It seems cruel of you to part our little prince from his milk brother, my lord."

Careful now, careful. "Mother's milk is all they share. Gilly's son is larger and more robust. He kicks the prince and pinches him, and shoves him from the breast. Craster was his father, a cruel man and greedy, and blood tells."

The king was confused. "I thought the wet nurse was this man Craster's *daughter?*"

"Wife and daughter both, Your Grace. Craster married all his daughters. Gilly's boy was the fruit of their union."

"Her own *father* got this child on her?" Stannis sounded shocked. "We are well rid of her, then. I will not suffer such abominations here. This is not King's Landing."

"I can find another wet nurse. If there's none amongst the wildlings, I will send to the mountain clans. Until such time, goat's milk should suffice for the boy, if it please Your Grace."

"Poor fare for a prince . . . but better than whore's milk, aye." Stannis drummed his fingers on the map. "If we may return to the matter of these forts . . ."

"Your Grace," said Jon, with chilly courtesy, "I have housed your men and fed them, at dire cost to our winter stores. I have clothed them so they would not freeze."

Stannis was not appeased. "Aye, you've shared your salt pork and porridge, and you've thrown us some black rags to keep us warm. Rags the wildlings would have taken off your corpses if I had not come north."

Jon ignored that. "I have given you fodder for your horses, and once the stair is done I will lend you builders to restore the Nightfort. I have even agreed to allow you to settle wildlings on the Gift, which was given to the Night's Watch in perpetuity."

"You offer me empty lands and desolations, yet deny me the castles I require to reward my lords and bannermen."

"The Night's Watch built those castles . . ."

"And the Night's Watch abandoned them."

" . . . to defend the Wall," Jon finished stubbornly, "not as seats for southron lords. The stones of those forts are mortared with the blood and bones of my brothers, long dead. I cannot give them to you."

"Cannot or will not?" The cords in the king's neck stood out sharp as swords. "I offered you a name."

"I have a name, Your Grace."

"Snow. Was ever a name more ill-omened?" Stannis touched his sword hilt. "Just who do you imagine that you are?"

"The watcher on the walls. The sword in the darkness."

"Don't prate your words at me." Stannis drew the blade he called Lightbringer. "*Here* is your sword in the darkness." Light rippled up and down the blade, now red, now yellow, now orange, painting the king's face in harsh, bright hues. "Even a green boy should be able to see that. Are you blind?"

"No, Sire. I agree these castles must be garrisoned—"

"The boy commander agrees. How fortunate."

"—by the Night's Watch."

"You do not have the men."

"Then give me men, Sire. I will provide officers for each of the abandoned forts, seasoned commanders who know the Wall and the lands beyond, and how best to survive the coming winter. In return for all we've given you, grant me the men to fill out the garrisons. Men-at-arms, crossbowmen, raw boys. I will even take your wounded and infirm."

Stannis stared at him incredulously, then gave a bark of laughter. "You are bold enough, Snow, I grant you that, but you're mad if you think my men will take the black."

"They can wear any color cloak they choose, so long as they obey my officers as they would your own."

The king was unmoved. "I have knights and lords in my service, scions of noble Houses old in honor. They cannot be expected to serve under poachers, peasants, and murderers."

Or bastards, Sire? "Your own Hand is a smuggler."

"*Was* a smuggler. I shortened his fingers for that. They tell me that you are the nine-hundred-ninety-eighth man to command the Night's Watch, Lord Snow. What do you think the nine-hundred-ninety-ninth might say about these castles? The sight of your head on a spike might inspire him to be more helpful." The king laid his bright blade down on the map, along the Wall, its steel shimmering like sunlight on water. "You are only lord commander by my sufferance. You would do well to remember that."

"I am lord commander because my brothers chose me." There were mornings when Jon Snow did not quite believe it himself, when he woke up thinking surely this was some mad dream. *It's like putting on new clothes,* Sam had told him. *The fit feels strange at first, but once you've worn them for a while you get to feeling comfortable.*

"Alliser Thorne complains about the manner of your choosing, and I cannot say he does not have a grievance." The map lay between them like a battleground, drenched by the colors of the glowing sword. "The count was done by a *blind man* with your fat friend by his elbow. And Slynt names you a turncloak."

And who would know one better than Slynt? "A turncloak would tell you what you wished to hear and betray you later. Your Grace knows that I was fairly chosen. My father always said you were a just man." *Just but harsh* had been Lord Eddard's exact words, but Jon did not think it would be wise to share that.

"Lord Eddard was no friend to me, but he was not without some sense. He would have given me these castles."

Never. "I cannot speak to what my father might have done. I took an oath, Your Grace. The Wall is mine."

"For now. We will see how well you hold it." Stannis pointed at him. "Keep your ruins, as they mean so much to you. I promise you, though, if any remain empty when the year is out, I will take them with your leave or without it. And if even one should fall to the foe, your head will soon follow. Now get out."

Lady Melisandre rose from her place near the hearth. "With your leave, Sire, I will show Lord Snow back to his chambers."

"Why? He knows the way." Stannis waved them both away. "Do what you will. Devan, food. Boiled eggs and lemon water."

After the warmth of the king's solar, the turnpike stair felt bone-chillingly cold. "Wind's rising, m'lady," the serjeant warned Melisandre as he handed Jon back his weapons. "You might want a warmer cloak."

"I have my faith to warm me." The red woman walked beside Jon down the steps. "His Grace is growing fond of you."

"I can tell. He only threatened to behead me twice."

Melisandre laughed. "It is his silences you should fear, not his words." As they stepped out into the yard, the wind filled Jon's cloak and sent it flapping against her. The red priestess brushed the black wool aside and slipped her arm through his. "It may be that you are not wrong about the wildling king. I shall pray for the Lord of Light to send me guidance. When I gaze into the flames, I can see through stone and earth, and find the truth within men's souls. I can speak to kings long dead and children not yet born, and watch the years and seasons flicker past, until the end of days."

"Are your fires never wrong?"

"Never . . . though we priests are mortal and sometimes err, mistaking *this must come* for *this may come.*"

Jon could feel her heat, even through his wool and boiled leather. The sight of them arm in arm was drawing curious looks. *They will be whispering in the barracks tonight.* "If you can truly see the morrow in your flames, tell me when and where the next wildling attack will come." He slipped his arm free.

"R'hllor sends us what visions he will, but I shall seek for this man Tormund in the flames." Melisandre's red lips curled into a smile. "I have seen you in my fires, Jon Snow."

"Is that a threat, my lady? Do you mean to burn me too?"

"You mistake my meaning." She gave him a searching look. "I fear that I make you uneasy, Lord Snow."

Jon did not deny it. "The Wall is no place for a woman."

"You are wrong. I have dreamed of your Wall, Jon Snow. Great was the lore that raised it, and great the spells locked beneath its ice. We walk beneath one of the hinges of the world." Melisandre gazed up at it, her breath a warm moist cloud in the air. "This is my place as it is yours, and soon enough you may have grave need of me. Do not refuse my friendship, Jon. I have seen you in the storm, hard-pressed, with enemies on every side. You have so many enemies. Shall I tell you their names?"

"I know their names."

"Do not be so certain." The ruby at Melisandre's throat gleamed red. "It is not the foes who curse you to your face that you must fear, but those who smile when you are looking and sharpen their knives when you turn your back. You would do well to keep your wolf close beside you. Ice, I see, and daggers in the dark. Blood frozen red and hard, and naked steel. It was very cold."

"It is always cold on the Wall."

"You think so?"

"I *know* so, my lady."

"Then you know nothing, Jon Snow," she whispered.

BRAN

Are we there yet?

Bran never said the words aloud, but they were often on his lips as their ragged company trudged through groves of ancient oaks and towering grey-green sentinels, past gloomy soldier pines and bare brown chestnut trees. *Are we near?* the boy would wonder, as Hodor clambered up a stony slope, or descended into some dark crevice where drifts of dirty snow cracked beneath his feet. *How much farther?* he would think, as the great elk splashed across a half-frozen stream. *How much longer? It's so cold. Where is the three-eyed crow?*

Swaying in his wicker basket on Hodor's back, the boy hunched down, ducking his head as the big stableboy passed beneath the limb of an oak. The snow was falling again, wet and heavy. Hodor walked with one eye frozen shut, his thick brown beard a tangle of hoarfrost, icicles drooping from the ends of his bushy mustache. One gloved hand still clutched the rusty iron longsword he had taken from the crypts below Winterfell, and from time to time he would lash out at a branch, knocking loose a spray of snow. "Hod-d-d-dor," he would mutter, his teeth chattering.

The sound was strangely reassuring. On their journey from Winterfell to the Wall, Bran and his companions had made the miles shorter by talking and telling tales, but it was different here. Even Hodor felt it. His *hodors* came less often than they had south of the Wall. There was a stillness to this wood like nothing Bran had ever known before. Before the snows began, the north wind would swirl around them and clouds of dead brown leaves would kick up from the ground with a faint small rustling sound that reminded him of roaches scurrying in a cupboard, but now all the leaves were buried under a blanket of white. From time to time a raven would fly overhead, big black wings slapping against the cold air. Elsewise the world was silent.

Just ahead, the elk wove between the snowdrifts with his head down, his huge rack of antlers crusted with ice. The ranger sat astride his broad back, grim and silent. *Coldhands* was the name that the fat boy Sam had given him, for though the ranger's face was pale, his hands were black and hard as iron, and cold as iron too. The rest of him was wrapped in layers of wool and boiled leather and ringmail, his features shadowed by his hooded cloak and a black woolen scarf about the lower half of his face.

Behind the ranger, Meera Reed wrapped her arms around her brother, to shelter him from the wind and cold with the warmth of her own body. A crust of frozen snot had formed below Jojen's nose, and from time to time he shivered violently. *He looks so small*, Bran thought, as he watched him sway. *He looks smaller than me now, and weaker too, and I'm the cripple.*

Summer brought up the rear of their little band. The direwolf's breath frosted the forest air as he padded after them, still limping on the hind leg that had taken the arrow back at Queenscrown. Bran felt the pain of the old wound whenever he slipped inside the big wolf's skin. Of late Bran wore Summer's body more often than his own; the wolf felt the bite of the cold, despite the thickness of his fur, but he could see farther and hear better and smell more than the boy in the basket, bundled up like a babe in swaddling clothes.

Other times, when he was tired of being a wolf, Bran slipped into Hodor's skin instead. The gentle giant would whimper when he felt him, and thrash his shaggy head from side to side, but not as violently as he had the first time, back at Queenscrown. *He knows it's me*, the boy liked to tell himself. *He's used to me by now.* Even so, he never felt comfortable inside Hodor's skin. The big stableboy never understood what was happening, and Bran could taste the fear at the back of his mouth. It was better inside Summer. *I am him, and he is me. He feels what I feel.*

Sometimes Bran could sense the direwolf sniffing after the elk, wondering if he could bring the great beast down. Summer had grown accustomed to horses at Winterfell, but this was an elk and elk were prey. The direwolf could sense the warm blood coursing beneath the elk's shaggy hide. Just the smell was enough to make the slaver run from between his jaws, and when it did Bran's mouth would water at the thought of rich, dark meat.

From a nearby oak a raven *quork*ed, and Bran heard the sound of wings as another of the big black birds flapped down to land beside it. By day only half a dozen ravens stayed with them, flitting from tree to tree or riding on the antlers of the elk. The rest of the murder flew ahead or lingered behind. But when the sun sank low they would return, descending from the sky on night-black wings until every branch of every tree was thick with them for yards around. Some would fly to the ranger and mutter at him, and it seemed to Bran that he understood their *quorks* and *squawks*. *They are his eyes and ears. They scout for him, and whisper to him of dangers ahead and behind.*

As now. The elk stopped suddenly, and the ranger vaulted lightly from his back to land in knee-deep snow. Summer growled at him, his fur bristling. The direwolf did not like the way that Coldhands smelled. *Dead meat, dry blood, a faint whiff of rot. And cold. Cold over all.*

"What is it?" Meera wanted to know.

"Behind us," Coldhands announced, his voice muffled by the black wool scarf across his nose and mouth.

"Wolves?" Bran asked. They had known for days that they were being followed. Every night they heard the mournful howling of the pack, and every night the wolves seemed a little closer. *Hunters, and hungry. They can smell how weak we are.* Often Bran woke shivering hours before the dawn, listening to the sound of them calling to one another in the distance as he waited for the sun to rise. *If there are wolves, there must be prey,* he used to think, until it came to him that *they* were the prey.

The ranger shook his head. "Men. The wolves still keep their distance. These men are not so shy."

Meera Reed pushed back her hood. The wet snow that had covered it tumbled to the ground with a soft *thump*. "How many men? Who are they?"

"Foes. I'll deal with them."

"I'll come with you."

"You'll stay. The boy must be protected. There is a lake ahead, hard frozen. When you come on it, turn north and follow the shoreline. You'll come to a fishing village. Take refuge there until I can catch up with you."

Bran thought that Meera meant to argue until her brother said, "Do as he says. He knows this land." Jojen's eyes were a dark green, the color of moss, but heavy with a weariness that Bran had never seen in them before. *The little grandfather.* South of the Wall, the boy from the crannogs had seemed to be wise beyond his years, but up here he was as lost and frightened as the rest of them. Even so, Meera always listened to him.

That was still true. Coldhands slipped between the trees, back the way they'd come, with four ravens flapping after him. Meera watched him go, her cheeks red with cold, breath puffing from her nostrils. She pulled her hood back up and gave the elk a nudge, and their trek resumed. Before they had gone twenty yards, though, she turned to glance behind them and said, "*Men,* he says. What men? Does he mean wildlings? Why won't he say?"

"He said he'd go and deal with them," said Bran.

"He *said,* aye. He said he would take us to this three-eyed crow too. That river we crossed this morning is the same one we crossed four days ago, I swear. We're going in circles."

"Rivers turn and twist," Bran said uncertainly, "and where there's lakes and hills, you need to go around."

"There's been too much *going around,*" Meera insisted, "and too many secrets. I don't like it. I don't like *him.* And I don't trust him. Those hands of his are bad enough. He hides his face, and will not speak a name. Who is he? *What* is he? Anyone can put on a black cloak. Anyone, or any *thing.* He does not eat, he never drinks, he does not seem to feel the cold."

It's true. Bran had been afraid to speak of it, but he had noticed. Whenever they took shelter for the night, while he and Hodor and the Reeds huddled together for warmth, the ranger kept apart. Sometimes Coldhands closed his eyes, but Bran did not think he slept. And there was something else . . .

"The scarf." Bran glanced about uneasily, but there was not a raven to be seen. All the big black birds had left them when the ranger did. No one was listening. Even so, he kept his voice low. "The scarf over his mouth, it never gets all hard with ice, like Hodor's beard. Not even when he talks."

Meera gave him a sharp look. "You're right. We've never seen his breath, have we?"

"No." A puff of white heralded each of Hodor's *hodor*s. When Jojen or his sister spoke, their words could be seen too. Even the elk left a warm fog upon the air when he exhaled.

"If he does not breathe . . ."

Bran found himself remembering the tales Old Nan had told him when he was a babe. *Beyond the Wall the monsters live, the giants and the ghouls, the stalking shadows and the dead that walk,* she would say, tucking him in beneath his scratchy woolen blanket, *but they cannot pass so long as the Wall stands strong and the men of the Night's Watch are true. So go to sleep, my little Brandon, my baby boy, and dream sweet dreams. There are no monsters here.* The ranger wore the black of the Night's Watch, but what if he was not a man at all? What if he was some monster, taking them to the other monsters to be devoured?

"The ranger saved Sam and the girl from the wights," Bran said, hesitantly, "and he's taking me to the three-eyed crow."

"Why won't this three-eyed crow come to us? Why couldn't *he* meet us at the Wall? Crows have wings. My brother grows weaker every day. How long can we go on?"

Jojen coughed. "Until we get there."

They came upon the promised lake not long after, and turned north as the ranger had bid them. That was the easy part.

The water was frozen, and the snow had been falling for so long that Bran had lost count of the days, turning the lake into a vast white wilderness. Where the ice was flat and the ground was bumpy, the going was easy, but where the wind had pushed the snow up into ridges, sometimes it was hard to tell where the lake ended and the shore began. Even the trees were not as infallible a guide as they might have hoped, for there were wooded islands in the lake, and wide areas ashore where no trees grew.

The elk went where he would, regardless of the wishes of Meera and Jojen on his back. Mostly he stayed beneath the trees, but where the shore curved away westward he would take the more direct path across the frozen lake, shouldering through snowdrifts taller than Bran as the ice crackled underneath his hooves. Out there the wind was stronger, a cold north wind that howled across the lake, knifed through their layers of wool and leather, and set them all to shivering. When it blew into their faces, it would drive the snow into their eyes and leave them as good as blind.

Hours passed in silence. Ahead, shadows began to steal between the trees, the long fingers of the dusk. Dark came early this far north. Bran had come to dread that. Each day seemed shorter than the last, and where the days were cold, the nights were bitter cruel.

Meera halted them again. "We should have come on the village by now." Her voice sounded hushed and strange.

"Could we have passed it?" Bran asked.

"I hope not. We need to find shelter before nightfall."

She was not wrong. Jojen's lips were blue, Meera's cheeks dark red. Bran's own face had gone numb. Hodor's beard was solid ice. Snow caked his legs almost to the knee, and Bran had felt him stagger more than once. No one was as strong as Hodor, no one. If even his great strength was failing . . .

"Summer can find the village," Bran said suddenly, his words misting in the air. He did not wait to hear what Meera might say, but closed his eyes and let himself flow from his broken body.

As he slipped inside Summer's skin, the dead woods came to sudden life. Where before there had been silence, now he heard: wind in the trees, Hodor's breathing, the elk pawing at the ground in search of fodder. Familiar scents filled his nostrils: wet leaves and dead grass, the rotted carcass of a squirrel decaying in the brush, the sour stink of man-sweat, the musky odor of the elk. *Food. Meat.* The elk sensed his interest. He turned his head toward the direwolf, wary, and lowered his great antlers.

He is not prey, the boy whispered to the beast who shared his skin. *Leave him. Run.*

Summer ran. Across the lake he raced, his paws kicking up sprays of snow behind him. The trees stood shoulder to shoulder, like men in a battle line, all cloaked in white. Over roots and rocks the direwolf sped, through a drift of old snow, the crust crackling beneath his weight. His paws grew wet and cold. The next hill was covered with pines, and the sharp scent of their needles filled the air. When he reached the top, he turned in a circle, sniffing at the air, then raised his head and howled.

The smells were there. Mansmells.

Ashes, Bran thought, *old and faint, but ashes.* It was the smell of burnt wood, soot, and charcoal. A dead fire.

He shook the snow off his muzzle. The wind was gusting, so the smells were hard to follow. The wolf turned this way and that, sniffing. All around were heaps of snow and tall trees garbed in white. The wolf let his tongue loll out between his teeth, tasting the frigid air, his breath misting as snowflakes melted on his tongue. When he trotted toward the scent, Hodor lumbered after him at once. The elk took longer to decide, so Bran returned reluctantly to his own body and said, "That way. Follow Summer. I smelled it."

As the first sliver of a crescent moon came peeking through the clouds, they finally stumbled into the village by the lake. They had almost walked straight through it. From the ice, the village looked no different than a dozen other spots along the lakeshore. Buried under drifts of snow, the round stone houses could just as easily have been boulders or hillocks or fallen logs, like the deadfall that Jojen had mistaken for a building the day before, until they dug down into it and found only broken branches and rotting logs.

The village was empty, abandoned by the wildlings who had once lived there, like all the other villages they had passed. Some had been burned, as if the inhabitants had wanted to make certain they could not come creeping back, but this one had been spared the torch. Beneath the snow they found a dozen huts and a longhall, with its sod roof and thick walls of rough-hewn logs.

"At least we will be out of the wind," Bran said.

"Ho*dor*," said Hodor.

Meera slid down from the elk's back. She and her brother helped lift Bran out of the wicker basket. "Might be the wildlings left some food behind," she said.

That proved a forlorn hope. Inside the longhall they found the ashes of a fire, floors of hard-packed dirt, a chill that went bone deep. But at least they had a roof above their heads and log walls to keep the wind off. A stream ran nearby, covered with a film of ice. The elk had to crack it with his hoof to drink. Once Bran and Jojen and Hodor were safely settled, Meera fetched back some chunks of broken ice for them to suck on. The melting water was so cold it made Bran shudder.

Summer did not follow them into the longhall. Bran could feel the big wolf's hunger, a shadow of his own. "Go hunt," he told him, "but you leave the elk alone." Part of him was wishing he could go hunting too. Perhaps he would, later.

Supper was a fistful of acorns, crushed and pounded into paste, so bitter that Bran gagged as he tried to keep it down. Jojen Reed did not even make the attempt. Younger and frailer than his sister, he was growing weaker by the day.

"Jojen, you have to eat," Meera told him.

"Later. I just want to rest." Jojen smiled a wan smile. "This is not the day I die, sister. I promise you."

"You almost fell off the elk."

"Almost. I am cold and hungry, that's all."

"Then eat."

"Crushed acorns? My belly hurts, but that will only make it worse. Leave me be, sister. I'm dreaming of roast chicken."

"Dreams will not sustain you. Not even greendreams."

"Dreams are what we have."

All we have. The last of the food that they had brought from the south was ten days gone. Since then hunger walked beside them day and night. Even Summer could find no game in these woods. They lived on crushed acorns and raw fish. The woods were full of frozen streams and cold black lakes, and Meera was as good a fisher with her three-pronged frog spear as most men were with hook and line. Some days her lips were blue with cold by the time she waded back to them with her catch wriggling on her tines. It had been three days since Meera caught a fish, however. Bran's belly felt so hollow it might have been three years.

After they choked down their meagre supper, Meera sat with her back against a wall, sharpening her dagger on a whetstone. Hodor squatted down beside the door, rocking back and forth on his haunches and muttering, "Hodor, hodor, hodor."

Bran closed his eyes. It was too cold to talk, and they dare not light a fire. Coldhands had warned them against that. *These woods are not as empty as you think,* he had said. *You cannot know what the light might summon from the darkness.* The memory made him shiver, despite the warmth of Hodor beside him.

Sleep would not come, could not come. Instead there was wind, the biting cold, moonlight on snow, and fire. He was back inside Summer, long leagues away, and the night was rank with the smell of blood. The scent was strong. *A kill, not far.* The flesh would still be warm. Slaver ran between his teeth as the hunger woke inside him. *Not elk. Not deer. Not this.*

The direwolf moved toward the meat, a gaunt grey shadow sliding from tree to tree, through pools of moonlight and over mounds of snow. The wind gusted around him, shifting. He lost the scent, found it, then lost it again. As he searched for it once more, a distant sound made his ears prick up.

Wolf, he knew at once. Summer stalked toward the sound, wary now. Soon enough the scent of blood was back, but now there were other smells: piss and dead skins, bird shit, feathers, and wolf, wolf, wolf. *A pack.* He would need to fight for his meat.

They smelled him too. As he moved out from amongst the darkness of the trees into the bloody glade, they were watching him. The female was chewing on a leather boot that still had half a leg in it, but she let it fall at his approach. The leader of the pack, an old male with a grizzled white muzzle and a blind eye, moved out to meet him, snarling, his teeth bared. Behind him, a younger male showed his fangs as well.

The direwolf's pale yellow eyes drank in the sights around them. A nest of entrails coiled through a bush, entangled with the branches. Steam rising from an open belly, rich with the smells of blood and meat. A head staring sightlessly up at a horned moon, cheeks ripped and torn down to bloody bone, pits for eyes, neck ending in a ragged stump. A pool of frozen blood, glistening red and black.

Men. The stink of them filled the world. Alive, they had been as many as the fingers on a man's paw, but now they were none. *Dead. Done. Meat.* Cloaked and hooded, once, but the wolves had torn their clothing into pieces in their frenzy to get at the flesh. Those who still had faces wore thick beards crusted with ice and frozen snot. The falling snow had begun to bury what remained of them, so pale against the black of ragged cloaks and breeches. *Black.*

Long leagues away, the boy stirred uneasily.

Black. Night's Watch. They were Night's Watch.

The direwolf did not care. They were meat. He was hungry.

The eyes of the three wolves glowed yellow. The direwolf swung his head from side to side, nostrils flaring, then bared his fangs in a snarl. The younger male backed away. The direwolf could smell the fear in him. *Tail,* he knew. But the one-eyed wolf answered with a growl and moved to block his advance. *Head. And he does not fear me though I am twice his size.*

Their eyes met.

Warg!

Then the two rushed together, wolf and direwolf, and there was no more time for thought. The world shrank down to tooth and claw, snow flying as they rolled and spun and tore at one another, the other wolves snarling and snapping around them. His jaws closed on matted fur slick with hoarfrost, on a limb thin as a dry stick, but the one-eyed wolf clawed at his belly and tore himself free, rolled, lunged for him. Yellow fangs snapped closed on his throat, but he shook off his old grey cousin as he would a rat, then charged after him, knocked him down. Rolling, ripping, kicking, they fought until the both of them were ragged and fresh blood dappled the snows around them. But finally the old one-eyed wolf lay down and showed his belly. The direwolf snapped at him twice more, sniffed at his butt, then lifted a leg over him.

A few snaps and a warning growl, and the female and the tail submitted too. The pack was his.

The prey as well. He went from man to man, sniffing, before settling on the biggest, a faceless thing who clutched black iron in one hand. His other hand was missing, severed at the wrist, the stump bound up in leather. Blood flowed thick and sluggish from the slash across his throat. The wolf lapped at it with his tongue, licked the ragged eyeless ruin of his nose and cheeks, then buried his muzzle in his neck and tore it open, gulping down a gobbet of sweet meat. No flesh had ever tasted half as good.

When he was done with that one, he moved to the next, and devoured the choicest bits of that man too. Ravens watched him from the trees, squatting dark-eyed and silent on the branches as snow drifted down around them. The other wolves made do with his leavings; the old male